THE LAST NIGHT

Cover Design: Brandon Wells

Published by Kendra Henderson

Copyright © 2024 by Kendra Henderson

Second Edition, October 2025

Printed in the United States of America

ISBN: 9798993581118

THE

THE
LAST NIGHT
KENDRA HENDERSON

I dedicate this book to my husband Kevin, who has always supported me through my writing journey, and to my children, who have always believed in me.

She believed she could, so she did.

– Scoring Wilder, R.S. Grey

PROLOGUE

—

Today, my stomach feels bad. It feels like I have little spiders crawling everywhere. I feel like I have to throw up, but nothing is coming out.

It's report card day, and I can't imagine what my grades are going to be. I'm only in the eighth grade at this point, but I'm always under so much pressure that I feel like I'm already in college. I feel this way, thanks to my mother.

She doesn't understand that a "C" is just as good of a grade as any other. To me, at least, I'm not failing. School is hard, if you ask me, especially growing up in a town like this.

Yesterday, I got whipped in front of my entire class. The teachers here can spank us for whatever reason they felt that justified the need for one. I hate it here.

As I sat in class, waiting for my teacher to pull out that stack of white envelopes, I began to bite my nails in fear. I could feel my palms getting sweaty and my knees starting to tremble. I was afraid of seeing what big, bold letters would be printed on my report card this time.

This was it for me. I know I'll be greeted with a slap in the face once I get home. I know as I walk down the street from the bus, I'll be stared at by those in town as if I'm walking on death row.

My mother has never been the nurturing type. She's always been big on appearance. If my siblings and I made her look bad in any way, she would torture us.

On days when our mother wasn't around, my sister Sarah and I would run off and hide in our house to play pretend. It wasn't the normal pretend play that most kids experience at our age. We would pretend we were leaving our town.

My sister loves horses, and she would always pretend to ride off in the sunset and never come back. I didn't care for horses much, but if that was the only way out of here, I was okay with the idea of riding off with her. It didn't matter to me how I got out of here as long as I did.

Our brothers Cameron and James were our mother's favorite. They barely got any beatings. Our oldest brother, Cameron, loved to see us get in trouble, so he would lie on my sister and me to witness whatever torture our mother would put us through.

"Alice! Alice!" Shoot, my teacher caught me daydreaming in class. Well, I can tell you now that this will be a cause for punishment.

"Yes ma'am, I'm sorry. I was thinking... it really doesn't matter." I told my teacher as she stared at me with fire in her eyes.

"Take this envelope home and make sure your mom signs this. Do not open it at all. This is for your mother, and she is the only one who can open it," my teacher instructed me.

What kind of crap is that? I thought to myself. Why can't I open my own report card? Shouldn't I be able to see what kind of punishment I'll need to prepare myself for once my mother looks at this tiny piece of paper that will determine my fate?

I can see it now. I'll be hiding under my bed again from trying to escape my mom's wrath. I guess I'll prepare myself for whatever I have to come.

Once school was over and the bus dropped me off at the bus stop, I was very nervous as I walked home. In fact, I was terrified. Why can't my mother be like the moms you see on television who will say, "It's okay, Alice. You need to try harder next time." But no, not my mom.

I finally made it to the front door. I turned the knob slowly to open the door, and there she was, standing right before me, wearing her yellow blouse and white skirt, staring at me with her dark brown eyes. Man, if eyes could kill, I would be dead by now. I knew something was wrong because she stood there with her hands on her hips. She only stands like that when something is wrong. She looked pissed. She looked like she was ready to rip me apart.

"Hey, Mom, I got my report card today," I immediately told her as I walked into the house.

"Well, give it here, child," she said to me. I didn't get one greeting from her. How about,

"Hey, sweetie, that's good to hear. Hug me first." She also could have said, "Oh, that's nice, dear, but first, would you like some cookies?" I desperately wanted love from this lady, but it would never happen.

I handed her my report card with trembling hands and waited anxiously as she looked at my letter grade for this quarter. Unsure of what her reaction would be, I slowly set down my backpack, preparing myself to run if necessary.

"Well, Alice, it looks like you're not as dumb as I thought," my mother told me. Believe it or not, I was thrilled to hear her say that. That's very sad, I know, but those words assured me that I must have received a grade that was to her liking.

Just when I thought I was home free from getting tortured today, the phone rang. "Hello." My mother answered the phone.

"Oh, really? She did what today in class? Well, thank you for informing me of her behavior. I'll make sure this never happens again."

My mom turned around, and at this point, I knew what was about to happen. It was like I went from looking at a somewhat sane person to looking the devil right in her eyes.

"Your teacher just called and stated you were daydreaming in class," my mother told me. "You know how I feel about being embarrassed. Are you trying to embarrass me, Alice?"

"No ma'am, I wasn't trying to embarrass you at all. I was thinking about my grade and what I could have possibly gotten this time. I just wanted to make you happy, Mom." I said to her with tears rolling down my cheeks.

"Make me happy?" She reiterated as she continued to move closer and closer to me.

As I stood there, I knew something terrible was getting ready to happen. I begged her not to hurt me and to give me another chance. My mother wasn't trying to hear my pleas. She already had her mind made up what she was getting ready to do.

In the blink of an eye, she quickly grabbed her leather belt and swung it across my face. My nose was bleeding at this point, and my face felt as if it was on fire. "MOM PLEASE STOP!" I screamed as she continued to swing the belt at me. She didn't care what part of my body she hit;

she just continued to swing.

"Alice, I'm doing this because I love you," she said as she continued to hit me. "The only way you are going to learn is if I beat it out of you."

Finally, she took a brief break, which was my chance to escape. I immediately took off running up the stairs. *Oh God, please don't let her catch me.*

Our house is extremely big, it has many rooms; honestly, I don't think she knows her way around properly. Apparently, our grandparents left it to our mom when they died. From my understanding, they were pretty loaded. They invented some filtration tablet for the city's water.

My sister and I found a room that was completely abandoned. Honestly, you would think someone had died in that room, but my sister and I didn't care. Our mother never stepped foot in this room, so this was our secret place.

I could feel my heart racing as I made my way to our secret hideout. Sliding under the bed, I focused on controlling my breathing. I couldn't afford to make a sound, so I firmly pressed my hands over my mouth. Unsure of how long I would have to stay hidden, I thought to myself, *as angry as my mother is right now, I might be here all night.*

Laying there silently, I could hear my mom opening several room doors. I could hear her saying, "Alice, where are you? Are we really going to play hide and seek today? You already know Mommy doesn't want to play this game today. Come out, sweetheart."

She does this when she wants to find us. She thinks that saying nice things will manipulate me and cause me to come out and trust her. But I've been dealing with this long enough to know her. She will take another swing at me as soon as I come out.

Continuing to lay there, I finally heard footsteps approaching the room I was hiding in. I was certain my mother wouldn't enter this room, but I was wrong this time.

I could hear the door creep open and the sound of her heels stepping across the wooden floorboards. I still felt I was safe, though. I continued to hold my hand across my mouth to keep from making a sound. I swear, some days, it felt like she had elephant ears. She could hear us breathing from a mile away.

She wasn't going to find me this time, though. She doesn't even know we know about this room. There are a lot of places my sister and I have discovered in this house.

I continued to lie there silently as I heard her searching through the closet. Finally, her feet got closer and closer to the bed. I was scared at this point. She was a little too close for comfort if you ask me.

She wasn't moving at all. I could only imagine what she was thinking. *God, please don't let her find me.*

No mother should ever make her child fear them this bad. I was terrified of our mother, and some days, I felt she was even capable of killing me if she got mad enough. Laying there in silence, waiting for my mother to leave the room, I promised myself that I would leave this town the first chance I got and that I would never treat my kids this way.

CHAPTER 1

As I reminisced about the past, I would have never thought 20 years would have gone by this fast. I have never forgotten the promise I made to myself the night I was hiding under the bed. Finally, I have enough money saved up so that I could afford to escape this place.

I never thought this day would come—the day when I would be leaving this treacherous town. Who names their town Shallow Hale anyway? This town is so small; the population is only 500.

The biggest city closest to us is Atlanta. Why didn't our parents think of moving us there? I mean, there is so much more to do in Atlanta. If I'm being honest, if I were a person visiting Georgia, I would have never, in a million years, thought a town as small as ours could even exist.

We never got to visit Atlanta, though. We always got excuses that it was too far. From what I was told, it's only a little under an hour away, so why were we always confined here?

Now that I'm older, you would think I would take the time to travel and maybe venture off to a place like Atlanta, but no, I never did. Something always seemed to come up. It was either work-related or life in general that got in the way.

I'll never forget the day I planned a weekend vacation to Atlanta. It was in the fall, so hurricane season was in full swing. The forecast called for strong winds and heavy rain, but that wasn't out of the ordinary for Georgia. What was unusual was how the authorities wouldn't let anyone leave town. They said it was a safety precaution and that the governor had them close all major roads.

I swear it felt like I was a prisoner in this town.

This town is a place where every resident is familiar with each other, and privacy seems like a foreign concept. It's as though the cashier at the local grocery store has an uncanny insight into our lives, making it feel nearly impossible to keep anything to ourselves.

The teachers wielded the authority to use physical force against students for minor infractions, such as sneezing loudly. The environment was toxic, bringing out the worst in everyone and creating an atmosphere of fear and hostility.

My mother was the worst of them all. She thought more about her appearance than she did about her own kids. I'll never forget the day she complained about possibly ruining her perfectly manicured nails to beat us. To keep from messing them up, she would beat us with her favorite leather belt if we even dared to disobey her.

My mother always felt the need to call me a whore. She always told me how I made her look bad to the people in town because I had two kids out of wedlock. It wasn't my fault the guy I thought I knew turned out to be a jerk and mysteriously up and left one day.

It's funny that she would even say something like that to me. She is one to talk if you ask me.

Our father couldn't even stick around because of her.

For many years, our mother has lied to everyone in town and told them our father went missing while serving overseas. She couldn't face the fact that people would see her differently raising four children alone. The reality is that our father left and never looked back.

I could remember it like it was yesterday. He always told her how controlling she was, and he couldn't take another minute of it. The arguments always seemed to be about her parents, who we never got the chance to meet.

Our father never allowed our grandparents to be near us. It was weird if you ask me. What kind of parent doesn't let their own children meet their grandparents? My only thought was that they must have done something extremely horrific for our father to feel that strongly about it.

Every day it felt like this town was sucking the life out of me, and I can no longer stand it. This will be the last night I have to put a fake smile on my face to avoid the confrontation I would have with my family. This will be the last night I have to see my horrible brothers and be a part of this god-forsaken family.

Every day I wake up here, it feels like bats are flying around in my stomach. I hate that I must walk around my town like I'm walking on eggshells. I dreamt of the next day because I knew that once this night was over, I would be free of this place, and my kids would not have to grow up feeling like I did.

I've finally found a place where my kids, Adam and Kandice, can live freely. Adam was never able to be himself here. He loved his video games and had his own sense of style, but the people in this town always had something to say about him. On several occasions, he would come home crying because someone took his game and threatened to break it if he didn't stop playing it in public.

This would be the last night my children and I would be residents of this awful town. This move wasn't just about me and my upbringing but about getting out of a town where no secret is kept hidden for long. As a kid, I could not walk the street without my neighbor already knowing what grades I got on my report card before I even made it home.

It was time for a change. I refused to allow my kids to grow up in a place where they would not be free to be themselves without someone forming their own opinion of them. I refused to allow them to come home another day with bruises because their teachers disagreed with their answers on the homework assignment they did the night before.

This town has a way with people, and I'm not saying it in a good way, but a way to make you want to either leave or commit suicide. I feel like a prisoner in this town; this will be the last night I have to feel this way again.

CHAPTER 2

—

Finally, the big day was here, and the movers were ready to load up our belongings. It wasn't like they had much to load. I had found the perfect house. It came fully loaded, so I didn't have to worry about furniture, which is a plus. I absolutely hated the idea of packing up all this furniture.

It was no surprise that all my family would be there as well. Everyone was covered in tears and pleading with me not to take the kids away. Hell would freeze over before I changed my mind about leaving this place.

My sister Sarah was the only person who was somewhat okay with my move. My mother, Lily-Ann, couldn't stop blaming me for her grandchildren's failure to grow up around their family because of how far away I was moving. But she could never understand that this move was best for me and my children. I would be able to provide them with a life I never had.

Inside me, I wanted to tell my mother to shove it and get over herself but to save my sanity; I decided to smile. To sacrifice my happiness and make this horrible person feel better, I hugged her as tightly as possible and said, "Mother, don't worry; you will see us again." I hoped this would make her shut up, but knowing my mother, it didn't.

She looked at me with an intense gaze. "Alice, you are so selfish; I will figure out how to convince the kids to return to me. I am their grandmother, by the way; who wouldn't want to be close to their grandmother?"

As always, she continued to find anything possible to say to make me feel like the horrible one in this situation.

Oh, Lily-Ann, if only you knew how much I despise you and only dreamt of the moment we would board the plane and never look back. At this point, she does not deserve to take on the title of a mother. Soon, my life will change, and I will never have to endure the pain and suffocation I feel every time I see her.

My sister was the only one who knew what was best for me. She's always talking about getting out herself one day. Whenever she got a fantastic job offer, she suddenly changed her mind and say, "There is so much history here, and it would be too hard to leave it all behind." I could never understand because, as kids, we always talked about leaving when we got old enough to get on our own feet.

On the other hand, our two brothers, Cameron and James, had different thoughts. Cameron never thought twice about leaving this dreadful place, and James always said yes to whatever Mother wanted. He never really had much of a say in anything around here.

Some days, I felt unfortunate for James because, in a way, he was like Sarah and me, being strung along by Lily-Ann in whatever way she deemed fit for her amusement. But James also knows right from wrong; some days, I could see when he felt our mother was wrong. But I could see right through James; he was always too afraid to say anything. He would go along as she demanded, even if that meant his two sisters would suffer.

Cameron was always the momma's boy. He always got his way with everything, while my sister and I always got his leftovers. He was the golden child in everyone's eyes, and this is why it was my time to leave. I remember when my mother made me and my sister sleep outside because my brother lied to Lily-Ann and told her we drank his juice and ate his favorite peach pie.

People go crazy around here over their peach pie. Georgia is the peach state; we have some of the best peaches. I heard stories of people coming from other states to try our peaches. But for Cameron to lie on my sister and me over some pie was preposterous, if you ask me.

What kind of parent makes their children sleep outside because of food? Not only was it horrible enough that we had to sleep outside, but it was also in the middle of winter. Our mother didn't even care to give us a blanket or pillow. Sarah and I had to snuggle up to keep warm and avoid frostbite.

Cameron always wanted to be an only child, and he knew he only had to tell a few lies to turn our mother against us. But that's okay. I'm moving on. I won't have to tell my kids about moments like this because our day is here, and it's time to leave all the bad memories behind.

After the movers left, my mother informed me that she invited a few family members to her house to wish the kids and me farewell. To my surprise, it was an actual party. This woman had thrown a going-away party for us. She has been holding these parties since I was born. From my understanding, it's been a tradition passed down from her parents. They held a party for everything. Your kid could have lost a tooth, and they would throw a party for it. In my opinion, rich people have nothing better to do but to blow their money.

One might assume that most people would be touched by such a thoughtful gesture, but not me. I couldn't help but question Lily-Ann's true motives behind this dinner party. It felt like a charade, a ploy to present herself as the most loving mother who would be inconsolable when her cherished child left.

At that moment, all I could think of was to spare me the torture Lily-Ann and just let us leave. I'd much rather sit at the airport for hours waiting to board my flight than sit here at this table contributing to your act. I'd much rather go through the somewhat of a security checkpoint they have than be your puppet today.

I know it is a surprise, but for a small town, we had a tiny airport with about four planes. As you can imagine, the entire town was there to wish us farewell. I continued to check the clocks, hoping this party would end any minute now, but like they say, time flies when you're having fun, and of course, I was more miserable than ever, so time went by, undoubtedly slowly.

My mother noticed my frustration, so she approached me with one of her expensive glasses filled with wine. I bet my life that she opened her 2015 bottle of Chateau Lafite Rothschild Pauillac red wine. She always has to have the best of the best.

"Here you are, sweetheart. I brought you

a glass of my best red wine," she said as she approached me.

How kind of her. Little did she know, I wasn't interested in taking anything from her. But I couldn't let her know that. So, I did what anyone else would do in my situation.

"Thanks Mom," I said with a smile on my face.

That wasn't enough for her to leave me alone. "So, what's the name of the city you're moving to again? What kind of person rents a fully furnished house? I mean, I really don't care for my grandkids sleeping and sitting on someone else's furniture."

My jaw dropped. You would think some of the things that come out of her mouth shouldn't surprise me, but she always finds a way to surprise me.

Taking a deep breath, I replied, "Really mother. This is what we are going to talk about right now?"

As she continued talking, she did what she'd been doing the whole time since I told her we were moving and tried to make me feel guilty for leaving once more.

"I don't have time for this. Aren't we supposed to be enjoying a party right now? Can we talk about that?" I asked with frustration in my voice.

She grabbed my face and squeezed my cheeks as tight as possible while digging her nails into my skin. Assuming this would be her last attempt to hold us hostage in her town, she leaned in close to me and whispered, "You will regret this move, trust me."

At this point, things were starting to get heated between us, so I snatched that expensive glass out of her hand and chugged my wine. After I got myself together, I said, "Mom, this is the last fight we will have because at 5 p.m., I'm out of this god-awful town, and you will not have to see my face again."

My mom responded with crocodile tears, as always: "Alice, it hurts me knowing you can leave and not look back at your home and family." She then wiped her tears, lifted her chin, and walked away.

CHAPTER 3

───

Heading to the airport, my sister told me about her dream of one day leaving Shallow Hale and opening her own horse stable. She's loved horses since she was a little girl. She would pretend with her stuffed animals that they lived in her stables, and she had people who worked with her and loved the horses just as much as she did. She would brush their hair and ensure they had the best horseshoes.

"I do admire you, Alice. Someday, I'll be just like you and leave this place. You're my hero, you know that, right?" Sarah said as she kept her focus on the road.

I hated leaving my sister behind, but now I have kids, which are my main priority.

Smiling at Sarah, I said, "You will trust me.

One day, you will get out of here and never look back."

"Do you remember that game we used to play? You know... the pretend game." Sarah asked.

How could I forget? It wasn't the regular pretend play normal kids do, where they dress up pretending to be a princess or a superhero. For us, it was more like pretending to leave our town.

I grabbed Sarah's right hand and gave it a light squeeze. "Yes, I can never forget that game."

Tears began to fall down her cheeks as I said that. Our mother has really screwed us up. My sister was scarred from our upbringing. But I couldn't understand why she still chose to stay here.

"Why haven't you left yet? I have two kids, so saving wasn't easy for me, but it's just you. So why stay?" I asked.

She quickly wiped her tears, glanced at me, and said, "Well, you know there is so much history here, and this is where we grew up. Why not stay?"

Typical answer. It almost felt rehearsed.

"Well, here we are. I will miss you Alice,"

Sarah said as she popped the trunk open so we could get our bags out. "Come here you two, give me a big hug and make sure you take care of your mom for me."

"I love you, Sarah. Take care of yourself and call me anytime." I say as I leaned in to hug her.

"Yeah, call us anytime, Auntie," Adam says as he struggles to put on his backpack, which is filled with every Nintendo game he owns.

Chuckling, Sarah gives Adam and Kandice a soft kiss on their foreheads.

I wasn't ready to say goodbye yet, so I turned around and gave my sister one last hug goodbye. Whispering in her ear, I say, "Once I get on my feet, I promise I'll come back for you and get you out of this hell hole."

Sarah gazed into my eyes as if she were telling me she knew I would do my best to come back for her. She grabbed my hands and gave them a light squeeze as she mouthed, "Thank you."

As my children and I walked shamefully through the airport, all the airport workers gave us the stare of death. It felt almost as if we were walking on death row. As I mentioned, there are no secrets in this town. Everyone knew I was leaving.

One of the airport attendants approached me as we walked by, "Doesn't this make you feel bad at all leaving your dear mother behind?" How could I answer that question? I absolutely do not feel bad. Little do these people know she is a wolf in sheep's clothing.

As we sat at our gate waiting to board the plane, I felt a glimpse of sadness. It felt like I was making a big mistake leaving my family like this. Lily-Ann's last words to me were, "I would regret this move." *What did she mean by that?*

Adam and Kandice knew me well enough to know when I was not having a good day. What helped me the most was knowing how proud they were of me for being brave enough to leave. I held them with a tight embrace, and the last tear this town would ever get out of me dropped on Adam's forehead.

He looked up at me with his thick, black, bushy hair and dark brown eyes and smiled at me. This wasn't any smile, but one with so much peace. One that assured us of a better, brighter future where we could be free from the town that bound them.

Finally, the call came for all guests to board Flight 209 to Oklahoma City. My heart pounded as I walked down the hall, holding my kids' hands to board the plane. They were thrilled for their first plane ride as we boarded.

On the inside, I was extremely nervous. We had never been on a plane, and I've seen so many movies of plane crashes or people taking over a plane. Unfortunately, this was the quickest way out of this hellhole of a town, so I ensured we were on the first flight out of there.

"Mom, is that where the pilot sits to fly the plane?" Adam asked as we walked past the cockpit.

"That's right buddy. That's called the cockpit. They close the doors so no one can get in." I responded.

"What! Why?" he asked as his eyes widened.

"Well, we don't want the pilot to be distracted, so once he goes in there, the doors lock, and only he can unlock them," I explained.

"Wow," he was amazed by my answer. But I

couldn't tell him the real reason why pilots lock the cockpit doors. Adam would have nightmares for days.

Once we located our seats, I started to feel a little tired. It was as if a wave of exhaustion just washed over me. Maybe my mother took all my energy during that last argument we had. I still don't understand what she meant when she said, "You will regret this move."

"Please put all bags in the overhead bins." The flight attendant instructed as she walked down the aisle.

We hurried to our seats as we noticed the flight attendants closing the overhead bins. From what I've seen on TV, this was their way of signaling that we were preparing for takeoff.

As I sat there staring out the tiny window, I noticed a small amount of what looked like steam coming from out the vent above us.

"Um, excuse me ma'am. What is that coming out the vent?" I asked one of the flight attendants as she walked by.

"Yes ma'am, that is just condensation. It's caused by the different temperatures from the outside air and the inside of the plane." She explained.

"Oh, thank goodness. This is our first time flying, and as you can see, I'm just a little nervous. I'm also a little nervous because I'm moving, and well... sorry, I tend to babble a lot when I'm nervous." I explain as I'm fiddling with my fingers.

Laughing at me, the flight attendant put her hand on my shoulder and assured me I had nothing to worry about. She told me this flight would be over before we knew it.

It was time for takeoff, and the flight attendants started to give the usual instructions on what to do in an emergency situation. Seeing my kids' faces light up as they saw us take off and be so high in the sky was going to be priceless. They were both so happy!

"Mom! Look, the plane is moving!" Adam said as he peeked out the window to see the runway.

"Duh, Adam, we are getting ready to take off. So that's what the plane is supposed to do." Kandice said while rolling her eyes.

Yawning, Adam looked at Kandice, "You don't always have to be such a smart aleck."

"Aww, is the baby getting sleepy?" Kandice said while also yawning.

"Come on you two, stop it. We are getting ready to be in a new place. Let's not start this new chapter of our lives off this way." I say while also yawning.

We must all have been very exhausted. The excitement of moving was taking a lot out of us.

Despite the anticipation of takeoff, I struggled to fight my sleep as we sat on the runway. The constant hum of the engines and the soothing vibrations of the aircraft were relaxing, and I fought to keep my eyelids from closing. I was determined to witness the sheer delight in the children's faces as the plane took off.

Slowly drifting, I heard the flight attendant announce, "This will be a three-hour flight, so please make yourself comfortable. We will be passing out complimentary snacks shortly."

With every ounce of my being, I fought to keep my eyes open, my gaze shifting to the kids. To my surprise, they had succumbed to sleep. I had been determined to stay awake and witness their excitement as we flew through the clouds, but now, I was also losing the battle against my exhaustion.

I slowly blinked my eyes and noticed the silhouette of a person standing in front of me. The flight attendant had mentioned that she was coming around with snacks, but I was too tired to eat at this point, so I lifted my hand to wave her off.

My eyelids couldn't take it anymore. It felt like I had two bricks holding them down. I had lost the battle, and I was officially out cold.

The pilot came on the intercom to explain that we will be landing in the next ten minutes. I woke up the kids so we could get our things together. We could hear the wheels coming from under the plane, and at this point, the kids and I were extremely excited about our new town. The seatbelt light came on, and we were ready to brace ourselves for the landing. It was a bit bumpy but absolutely worth it, knowing we were moving to a better place.

Stepping off the plane was like stepping into heaven. Everything looked different; even the airport was much better than the one in Shallow Hale. The kids were absolutely thrilled by the airport's plethora of restaurants and shops. Adam was ecstatic about the game store and was already declaring this place a major win in his book.

The people were very friendly, and everyone greeted us with a smile. As we continued through the airport, we were amazed that the state's governor was the one welcoming everyone who came in through this airport. All we could hear over the intercom was, "Welcome to Will Rogers World Airport here in Oklahoma City, Oklahoma. We are excited for all our travelers to be visiting this great state. Please stay awhile and enjoy our many extravagant restaurants and shops."

We gathered our things from baggage claim and headed for the rental car. Because it was so late and I was too tired to meet with anyone tonight, I recalled reading about a Holiday Inn across the street from the airport. I felt it was best that we got a room there for the night to get some sleep. We will have such a big day ahead of us tomorrow.

CHAPTER 4

—

O nce we checked into our room, instead of going straight to sleep, Adam and Kandice were full of questions. "Mom, what's the name of the town we're moving to?" Adam asked. "Mom, what's the name of our new school?" Kandice also asked.

"Guys, I know y'all are full of questions, but aren't you two tired? Can't these questions wait until tomorrow?" I begged them.

Adam, being the arrogant one that he is, only cares about becoming the most popular kid in school. He loves playing his games and trying to beat his highest score. He's always wanted to become a big-time YouTuber and attract many followers. For him, school was a place where he could promote his gaming talents.

On the other hand, Kandice didn't care so much about appearance or being the most popular kid in school. Her usual attire was baggy jeans, graphic t-shirts, and a pair of Nike dunks to match her outfit for that day. As long as the school had a library, she was happy. She is an avid reader and will get lost in a book any day.

It was hard to keep this vital piece of information from these two. They stared at me desperately, waiting for me to answer their questions. I couldn't hold back any longer. I reached over and grabbed my laptop from my bag to look up the information about the kid's school.

"So Adam, to answer your question, the town we are moving to is called Shelly Grove. From what I have read about the town, it looks like it's small, but according to Google, it's considered a safe place to live," I began to explain.

"It already sounds boring," Adam says as he rolls his eyes.

I chuckle at my son, "The town has three schools: an elementary school, a middle school, and a high school. From what I can see, the schools are named after the town, so you have Shelly Grove Elementary School, Shelly Grove Middle School, and Shelly Grove High School."

"Boring," Adam repeats himself.

"Shut up, let her talk," Kandice chimes in.

As I continued reading, I came across something I knew my daughter would enjoy. "It looks like there is a lot of greenery and trails to enjoy walks. They have several beautiful places to have picnics. A town park sits right in the middle of what is considered their downtown. From what I'm reading, this beautiful clock tower sits in the middle of the park."

"Now you're talking my language," Kandice adds.

Something else catches my eye as I continue my search, "Oh, this is interesting," I say. "A very tall hill sits on the edge of the town. Google says you can view the entire town if you hike to the top. I bet that is breathtaking. I can't wait to take a hike up there myself. It looks like several small shops are also there."

"Do they have a video game store?" Adam asks.

"Um...I don't think so," I hesitate to say. I want my kids to love the new town, and if a video game store is a deal breaker for my son, then maybe I should keep it to myself that they may not have one in a town like this.

"Mom, are you going to continue," Kandice asks.

"Oh yes, so according to Google, most of the people in town own these shops, which I bet makes for an interesting shopping experience," I add.

"Maybe one of those shops is a video game store!" Adam's eyes widen with excitement.

I chuckled. My son loves his video games. "Oh, and Kandice looks like they have a small movie theater. Once you start making friends, you can check out the theater. I'm sure that will be fun."

"Yeah, maybe," Kandice mutters.

After I explained to the kids what they could expect when we finally settled into our new place, Adam looked at me with his dark brown eyes and said, "Well, it looks like I got some work to do." I was very confused by his response.

"What do you mean you have some work to do?" I asked Adam.

"Well, Mom, the town sounds all right, but you mentioned nothing about a gaming lounge. There doesn't seem to be a place where younger kids can go to let loose, you know. Like there isn't anywhere, we can go play."

"I did mention a movie theater and a town park," I reminded him.

Adam scrunches his eyebrows, "You didn't say anything about an arcade room. You didn't say anything about a community pool. I mean, goodness, there isn't even a trampoline park."

I repeatedly remind him, "I did say there is a theater and a park. Also, when did you become an expert on entertainment venues? Back in our old town, we didn't have any of that stuff."

"Well, there is a thing called the internet, Mom. What is that saying people use? Seems like we are going from the pot to the skillet. Don't you think so, Kandice?" Adam asked.

Kandice replied, "I honestly don't care about that stuff, Adam. I think the place sounds great. I bet a park in the middle of downtown is really beautiful. Also, the hill that overlooks the entire town... I can't wait to see that either."

"Well, how about we just go to sleep, you two? We can debate all night about this town, but we won't get a good feel of it until we actually get there. If you ask me, the only way we will get there is if you two curious cats go to sleep," I say with a smile.

Both of them looked at me, and the debate was finally over. I think I actually won this round. They were finally ready to go to sleep, and I was extremely exhausted from all the travel. The bed never looked so good if you asked me.

CHAPTER 5

———

When we woke up that morning, the kids and I were eager to get to our new home. The kids couldn't finish their breakfast fast enough. As soon as we were done eating, Adam quickly ran back to our hotel room to gather his things.

"MOM COME ON LET'S GO!" Adam screamed as he continued to gather his belongings.

We were ready to start this new chapter of our lives as soon as we got our things together.

The stunning landscapes captivated our attention as we left the hotel to meet our new landlord. The 45-minute distance from the major city seemed insignificant as we were mesmerized by the surroundings. Leaving behind our small-town roots, I decided to reside outside the city, considering the favorable cost of living.

Moving to Shelly Grove was going to be life-changing. The kids were so excited about living in a new town, making new friends, and even more excited to meet their new teachers.

Throughout the drive, Adam and Kandice discussed what they would wear on their first day of school. The excitement was contagious because I felt just as ecstatic as they did. All I could think was, *if I had any doubts about this move, they were all gone now after seeing the twinkles in my kids' eyes.* This move was worth every penny.

As we entered the town of Shelly Grove, it seemed like the perfect place for a family. Kids were outside riding their bikes, and there were beautiful flowers everywhere. People were walking their dogs outside, and fathers were playing catch with their boys in the yard. The grass on every lawn was perfectly green, not one speck of brown in sight. The trees were perfect and very colorful; it was hard to believe a town like this even existed, considering where we moved from.

The small corner store was no longer the

town's shopping mall. They actually had a Walmart and a shopping center. There were no longer stop signs, but we had streetlights to control the intersections. This town really started to feel like home as we slowly drove through it, trying to find our subdivision.

We even had the opportunity to drive through downtown. The park was stunning. The grass was a vibrant green and fluffy, tempting me to stop my car and lie in it.

We saw the beautiful clock tower that we read about on the internet, and it was even more stunning in person. The tower, made entirely of brick, emitted a lovely chime. There was a space on the ground level where you could take photos or even have a wedding. It was the most beautiful sight I had ever seen.

As we pulled into the subdivision, the kids were excited to see where our new home was. They eagerly started counting the numbers on the houses until we finally pulled up to a beautiful, bright yellow house. It had everything we wanted in a home, including a big front porch with a swing. The kids and I could not believe our eyes. At that point, we felt like we had won the lottery and were definitely on cloud nine.

This was paradise for us. Our new place was one of those little houses with many windows and had the one window above the garage. As I stared at the house, I could only imagine all the memories we were getting ready to create in our home. I could picture Kandice sitting in that little window above the garage with her curly black hair pulled back in a ponytail. She would wear her usual baggy jeans and graphic T-shirt and read a nice book.

I could picture Adam wearing his everyday attire: a white T-shirt and sweatpants. These kids today are very funny, who wears a hoodie and sweatpants in the heat of summer. I could see him now, swinging on the front porch swing with his friends while playing his Nintendo Switch. Life is so good at this point, and I don't want this moment ever to end.

The temptation was killing the kids, and I could no longer hold them hostage. They were ready to get out of the car to explore their new home. We were startled by the front door opening as we slowly approached the house. We didn't notice a car parked in the driveway, so I figured no one was there yet. To my surprise, it was our landlord coming out to greet us.

She was the most beautiful woman I had ever seen for her age. She had the nicest clothes on and the darkest sunglasses. You couldn't even see her eyes. Very mysterious if you ask me. She had the tightest curls in her hair and the fanciest purse. It had to have cost a fortune.

She took off her hat and shook out her curls. Putting her hand out with her fancy nails, she introduced herself as Mrs. Sally. She explained to us how she and her husband pretty much own all the houses in this area. She was the sweetest lady and had the most heartwarming smile. She referred to my children as little sweethearts. Mrs. Sally was the sweetest little lady.

Remembering there was no car in the driveway, I asked, "Do you live nearby? I didn't see a car in the driveway."

"I see you are very observant," she says.

"Well, I kind of have to, with two kids, you know," I say with a chuckle.

"Right, well, my husband needed to run to the grocery store, so he dropped me off over here."

"Oh really?" I question.

"It's no big deal, dear. I don't want him hanging around while I do business. You know how men can be," she says with a chuckle.

"Well... what if I didn't show up?" I ask.

"Then I would have waited until he got back." She smiles.

"..."

"Well, don't just stand there dear. Come on in! Let's make this official so I can turn over the keys to this place to you," she said as she gestured for us to enter.

After the formalities of signing the papers, Mrs. Sally extended a invitation for brunch. Her persistence was endearing, and she left us with no choice but to accept The kids were naturally drawn to her, and their eagerness convinced me that a warm meal and a friendly face were exactly what we needed after a long journey.

As a parent, it's hard to resist your children's pleas, especially when they're asking to share a meal with the person who made this new home possible. So, we locked up the house and quickly headed towards the car.

"I just need to let my husband know I'm ready so he can pick me up. He isn't far." Mrs. Sally says.

"Don't be silly. You are welcome to ride with us. After all, you invited us to your house for breakfast, so the least we can do is offer you a ride," I say.

"If you insist, I'll just let him know to meet us at the house."

The drive to Mrs. Sally's house wasn't that far, which surprisingly gave me a little peace, knowing my landlord didn't live that far if I needed her help. Interestingly, her house was the only one in the town that wasn't in a subdivision, and it sat at the top of the hill alone. I'm assuming this is the hill Google was talking about.

When we arrived at her home, the view was nothing short of breathtaking. From this vantage point, we could see the entire town spread out before us with its houses and lush greenery. The thought of the view at night, with all the lights twinkling, was a promise of beauty yet to come.

You could also see the pretty clock tower from up here and hear the chime. This was the perfect view, in my opinion.

Once we approached the door, we were greeted by a man I assumed was Mrs. Sally's husband. He had the softest voice and kindest light brown eyes. He was the cutest little man with his salt-and-pepper-colored hair. He dressed just as good as she did. You could tell these two were loaded.

"Hello honey," Mrs. Sally said as the man opened the door. This is our new tenant, Alice, and her kids, Adam and Kandice."

"Hello Alice. It's a pleasure to meet you and the kids. I'm Mr. Gerald," he said, greeting us with a warm hug. "Please, come in. Sally informed me about your arrival, and I've prepared breakfast. It's almost ready."

That was fast. Wasn't he just at the store? I thought to myself.

He was a man of even greater sweetness than his wife. It was hard to believe that such people existed in this world. A sense of tranquility washed over me, a feeling I never experienced before. At that moment, I knew we had found our true home.

When Mr. Gerald escorted the kids and me to their spacious dining room, we were taken aback by the sight of the table overloaded with an assortment of foods. There was French toast, bacon, eggs, regular toast, sausage, grits, mixed fruit, yogurt, and various other dishes. The sheer variety and quantity made us wonder if this was a typical meal for these two. They even had water in crystal glass bottles. *Fancy*, I thought.

"This all looks very good, Mr. Gerald. Did you do all this yourself? I mean, you were just at the store. When did you have the time to prepare a meal this size?" I ask.

"Don't be silly, Gerald had some help. We do have a chef in the house." Mrs. Sally reassures me.

I nod my head slowly. *Now that makes perfect sense.* I thought to myself.

After breakfast, Mrs. Sally and Mr. Gerald gave us a grand tour of their lovely home and a breakdown of the town. It was such a pleasure getting to know them more, but sadly, time had flown, and it was time for us to leave. With all the insight they had given us about the town, we pretty much knew where the best donut shops were and, for the kids, where the movie theater was located.

As we walked through the living room heading for the front door, we noticed Mrs. Sally had a picture of her and another woman on her hallway table.

"Who is that, Mrs. Sally?" Adam asked.

"I'm so sorry; you know kids can be a little curious," I say.

She gently places a hand on Adam's shoulder and winks her eye at him. "Oh, he's fine dear. It's always good to ask questions. That's my daughter, Sam."

"Wow, you two could be twins!" Adam says excitedly.

Chuckling, she goes on to explain that her daughter also runs that amazing donut shop she told us about. Mrs. Sally spoke so highly of Sam that it felt as if I already had a best friend, and I hadn't even met her yet. It sounded like we had so much in common. I couldn't wait to meet her.

CHAPTER 6

The next day, it was time to get down to business and unpack our things. The kids had already picked their rooms and started declaring whose territory was whose. Suddenly, we heard a knock on the door.

Looking out the window, I saw this lady standing on the porch with a box. She was wearing capris-type jeans, a white T-shirt, and a light pink cardigan. She almost reminded me of a younger version of Mrs. Sally, except she didn't have tight curls. Her hair was pitch black, and she had it pulled back in a bun. She almost resembled a schoolteacher.

I opened the door, and the lady standing there stared at me briefly before saying anything. As I stared into her brown eyes, I could tell she was a little stunned—lost for words, if I must add.

Suddenly, the beautiful chime from the clock tower echoed through the town. I don't think I can ever get irritated by it. It's almost mesmerizing.

"How can I help you?" I asked as I stepped onto the front porch.

"Yes, I'm sorry. How rude of me. It's been a long morning if you ask me." The woman said with the sweetest voice. How could I be upset with her? She sounded like the character Miss Honey in the movie Matilda.

She smiled at me with the brightest white teeth and put her hand out to shake mine. "Hello, my name is... Sam. Mrs. Sally and Mr. Gerald are my parents," she stated. My mom told me about you and insisted I meet you. She also told me you had two kids, so I figured I would bring them a box of warm donuts from my shop."

"Oh my goodness, how did I miss it? Your mom showed us a picture of you when we were at her house yesterday. I don't know how I forgot that. You two look just alike." I say while chuckling.

"We get that all the time," she smiles and tucks a piece of straggling hair behind her ear.

It's a little weird for her to show up unexpectedly, but she brought donuts, so that's a serious game-changer for me.

"Come in, let's check out these donuts your mom talked so much about," I say.

After sitting down and talking with Sam for a few hours, it felt like we already knew each other and were long-lost friends. She was great; the kids immediately fell in love with her because she brought them donuts.

Sam and I realized we had a lot in common. She loved sweets just as much as I did. We also both enjoy taking hikes and gazing at beautiful scenery. We both loved the color purple, and we both were deathly afraid of snakes.

"Well, as much as I would love to continue our conversation, I really need to get back to unpacking," I told Sam.

Sam immediately chuckled and said, "Yes, I agree. These boxes aren't going to unpack themselves. As a matter of fact, I really don't have anything else going on for the rest of the day; I could stick around and lend a hand if you like."

Trying not to get overwhelmed with everything I had to do, I looked at Sam and said, "Well... I could use the help. The kids, of course, only cared about getting their rooms together. It would be nice to have someone else help me."

"Great! I can only imagine how you feel, having to unpack and not having much help. So, it's a good thing my mom had me come over. Let's get this place looking more like a home." Sam said as she smiled at me.

She was right about one thing. This place did not look like anyone had lived there yet. It was complete chaos. Boxes were everywhere.

I guess the only thing that helped was knowing I didn't have to put any furniture together. The house came fully furnished, just like the internet posting said. It was unbelievable.

The master bedroom came with a king-size bed that had a pillow-top mattress. There was also a cute little vanity that sat in the bathroom. The kids already had full-size beds and dressers. The kitchen had a cute little breakfast nook with a round table. The living room had two tan plush couches and a round coffee table directly in the middle of the floor. Really, the only thing we needed to do was unpack the boxes the mover dropped off for us from our old house.

While unpacking, Sam and I continued to chat. She asked me if I had found work yet. But the one question that stopped me in my tracks was what brought me and the kids all the way to Oklahoma?

"Well...I did find a little office assistant position working for a company here called TelNet. It's a phone and internet company. From what I read on Google, it looks like it is a small family-owned business." I informed her.

For a minute, I totally forgot all about home because this was our new home. I began to tell her we were from a small town with a population of about 500 people and how awful this town was. I explained to her that I had the worst upbringing.

"My mom...my mom...," I hesitate. I couldn't think of anything to say about her. But at this point, Sam was looking at me as if I had lost it. "You know what, it was just a horrible place, and the people there were just as bad."

Sam was shocked that a place like that could exist on this planet. Judging from where she grew up, I totally understand her feeling that way. Shelly Grove is like heaven on earth.

People are constantly outside playing with their kids. I hate the heat, but it doesn't seem to bother anyone here, with summer nearing. From what I can see, everyone is always smiling. The flowers are perfectly bloomed, and the grass is extremely green. You almost can't believe it's real.

Looking at the time, I realized it was getting late. "Man, time really does fly when you're having fun. Who would have thought unpacking a house would have been this much fun? But I have you to thank for that." I said to Sam.

Tomorrow was the kid's first day of school and my first day on the job. As much as I wasn't ready for her to leave, I knew the only way I would be ready for tomorrow was to go ahead and get to bed. I yelled for the kids to come down and say goodnight to Sam.

CHAPTER 7

———

I screamed at the top of my lungs, "KIDS, WAKE UP!" I rushed through the house, trying to keep track of the time to ensure we were all on time for our first day of school and work. I knew I would be prepared, but my sleep was slightly off last night.

I had the most unsettling dream. A tiny older woman wearing a pink sweater appeared in my room. She had gray curly hair and looked extremely frightened as she stood in the corner of my room. She kept repeating, "Leave, don't come back."

This dream was more than just a bad dream; it was a chilling warning. The harder I tried to wake up from it, the more it felt like I was trapped in a nightmare. It was as if I was drugged and couldn't escape this deep sleep. She was definitely trying to warn me about something.

With the thought of that dream on my mind and my alarm clock acting up, this morning is not starting off the way I had expected it. I couldn't find my shoes or the cardigan I wanted to wear on my first day. This was really weird.

I know I had all my clothes laid out last night.

This morning is starting off a little crazy as if someone didn't want me to have a good first day on the job. But forgetting about the outfit I intended to wear, I grabbed the next best thing, and the kids and I headed out the door.

Worried about our morning, I was unsure what to expect for the rest of our day. Was I going to get a flat tire? Were aliens going to come down and abduct me, causing me to miss my first day of work entirely? I wasn't sure what the rest of the day had in store for me, but I knew one thing for sure: I needed to hurry and get the kids to school before the first bell rang.

The clock tower resonated throughout the town as it chimed.

It was really cool hearing that as I took the

kids to school. It felt like it was a reminder for the people in town that it was school and work hours.

As we arrived at Adams school, even though he acted like a tough gaming kid, he still wanted me to walk him to the front door. Kandice, on the other hand, wouldn't dare be seen walking with her mom on her first day of school, so she had me drop her off in the carpool line at her school.

"Come on Mom, we're going to be late," Adam said as he quickly jumped out of the car.

I've never seen a child so eager for their first day of school.

Approaching the front of the school building, everyone in the carpool line got out of their cars simultaneously and hugged their kids goodbye. The kids who walked to school were escorted by their parents, who also hugged them goodbye.

"Interesting," I mumble.

"See Mom, aren't you glad you walked me to the door? Seems like that's what you are supposed to do around here." Adam said with a grin on his face.

"Right, I guess I didn't get that memo," I say

hesitantly.

Shaking off what I witnessed, I kissed Adam on his forehead and headed to work.

—  —

Surprisingly, the rest of the day went great, and my job was excellent. The people I worked with were fantastic; some of my coworkers set my office up for me to make it feel more personal for me. They put a few plants in my office, and someone even went as far as to put some fresh flowers on my desk. It was almost as if they already knew I was a sucker for plants and flowers. My boss, Mr. Crammer, was the best. He is a middle-aged, light-skinned man with curly black hair and dark brown eyes. From what everyone tells me, he likes to dress to impress. Today, he is wearing a light blue blazer, a white shirt, and khaki dress pants.

He even allows us to have casual Fridays. From what my coworkers told me, this was the best part of the work week. One of my coworkers told me he often takes all his employees out for a big lunch at his own expense.

Now I see why this place has a low turnaround

rate.

"Alice, as part of your onboarding process, could you please complete your new employee packet? Once you've finished this task, you're free to leave for the day," Mr. Crammer explained as he approached me.

First, I had my coworkers help decorate my office. Then I find out my boss pretty much gives out free lunches and now, he is telling me I can go home early on my first day. This was music to my ears, so I immediately began to fly through the packet until I came across the section for my emergency contact person.

I couldn't think of anyone that important to me to put down. As I sat there struggling, I looked up and noticed my boss staring at me. I tried my best to keep from looking confused, but he could tell something was up.

"Is there anything I can help you with Alice?" Mr. Crammer asked as he stepped back into my office.

With a stunned look on my face, I replied, "I can't think of anyone to put as my emergency contact."

"How about a family member? Are you married? Are your parents living? Do you have siblings?" he asked.

My mind went completely blank; I couldn't remember anything about my family. I knew I had a mother, father, and siblings, but I could not even picture their faces or remember their names. *As if my morning wasn't crazy enough.* I thought.

So that I would not look like an extremely insane person, I remembered Sam and that I had her contact information on my phone. I replied to him, "You know what? I'll just put a good friend of mine down; I know she would be a great emergency contact person."

When I had finished filling out the papers, I rushed home, given that I still had a few hours to spare before it was time for Adam and Kandice to get out of school. I ran into the house and started tearing open boxes still packaged up to find our family photos. Surprisingly, I could only find pictures of me and my kids. I checked my phone because I knew half my life was on this tiny computer, and to my surprise, the only images there were of the airport and pictures of our new home.

This was the weirdest thing, and I couldn't wrap my head around it. I sat down on the couch, speechless. I had no idea what was going on. I felt like I had just stepped into the twilight zone. The only explanation I could think of was maybe the time difference or the fact that I had turned my phone on and off on the airplane.

Technology has taken over most of our lives, so my entire life was on my phone. All I could think to myself was, *I know I have a family, but why on earth can't I remember them?* I had to remind myself that this move had taken a lot out of me, and maybe my memory would come back soon.

The clock tower echoed once again.

Oh goodness. I was startled by the chime from the clock tower. It was too quiet in this house. Looking down at my watch, I noticed it was 3 p.m.

That clock tower is really on target.

It was time to pick up the kids, so I had to get myself together and get ready to pick them up from school. I was so excited to hear what their first day of school was like. I read that this town has some of the best schools and the most loving teachers. This would be an excellent experience for both of them; I could feel it.

Once I made it to the kids' schools to pick them up, they both looked like they had the best day of their lives. Kandice began telling me how 8th grade is so cool and how their teachers allow them free time to use their phones. Adam, on the other hand, didn't care so much about 4th grade. He was only happy to meet a bunch of boys who liked video games just as much as he did.

As happy as I was to hear how much they loved the new school, I noticed something bothering Kandice, so I asked her what was on her mind.

Kandice went on to explain how her day went at school. She started with the moment she walked through the door; all eyes were on her. Slowly walking down the hall, she felt a little weirded out by all the attention, but she thought maybe this was how it was being the new kid there. As she walked into the front office, they immediately knew who she was and greeted her with a hug. Kandice explained at this point that the school had surpassed being weird; now, they were a little creepy.

Chuckling at her experience, I allowed her to continue explaining how her day went. She then said that as she gathered her things to be escorted to class, she looked over her shoulder and noticed the front office receptionist staring at her. I know teenagers can be extremely extra when telling a story, so I went along with what she was saying.

I explained to Kandice that maybe the front office lady was so happy to have a new student on board. She was always an honor roll student, so it could be that they were impressed with what she was going to bring to their school. Whatever the case, Kandice was being a bit dramatic, if you ask me.

Kandice knows when I am questioning the details of any story she tells. With a serious look, she says, "Mom, I know you don't believe me, but this school is a little creepy."

Looking at her, I knew it was time to put on a serious face. Something did startle Kandice about this school. As a mother, I can also see she is going through what I call new kid syndrome. But, sparing her feelings, I allowed her to continue telling us how her day went.

Kandice then explained how all the kids greeted her as she entered the classroom. She said it was as if she was the most popular girl in the school. Everyone excitedly jumped out of their seats and swarmed around her with a billion questions.

"Now Kandice, what is wrong with that?" I asked her. She said she had never seen a movie where all the kids were happy to see the new kid on the block.

I couldn't hold it in any longer. I laughed so hard at Kandice. She has no idea what it feels like to be in a different environment with sound, sensible kids. I wish I could have gone to a school like that as a kid. But it was hard for me to remember my school days for some odd reason.

From what Kandice told me, I couldn't understand why she said she had a good day when I picked them up from school. So I asked her to explain.

"Mom, I didn't want you to worry because

I know how much this move meant to you," she stated.

"What about you Adam? How was your first day?" I asked.

Adam is very different from Kandice; he loves attention. He explained that his morning was very similar to Kandice's. All the kids stared at him while he walked into the school, and the front office staff was ecstatic to see him as well. He never thought twice about it because he loves this kind of attention. He told us that when he walked into the classroom, the kids greeted him like they did Kandice at her school.

Adam enjoyed being the most popular kid for the day. Kandice asked him how he didn't think any of that was weird. But my son, oh my son, loves being the center of attention. He even told us one kid pulled out his chair so he could sit at his desk while another kid sharpened all his pencils.

Now I know my son, and he can make a story sound good. So I chuckled at the thought of kids really doing all that for him. Leaning his head against the headrest in the car, Adam said, "Yup

Mom, this is definitely the life."

Even though I was very excited to hear about their first day, it was still in the back of my mind that I couldn't remember who my family was. Maybe I'm losing it, or perhaps the trauma was so severe once we moved that my mind blocked it all out.

Who knows what's going on with me at this point? All that matters is the wonderful smiles on my kids' faces when we walked into our new home on our first day here. I know Kandice isn't feeling the new school at the moment, but it will grow on her. Seriously, what kid likes middle school anyway? This town seems like it is filled with so much love, so I know the school and the kids will eventually grow on her.

On our way home, we stopped by Sam's donut shop because the kids had fallen completely in love with her homemade donuts. As we sat there while the kids told Sam all about their day, I still couldn't stop thinking about my family.

I noticed Sam's gaze on me, her eyes piercing through my soul. She clearly could sense my unease, that something was troubling me.

THE LAST NIGHT

"Hey! So, how was your first day of work?" Sam asked.

"Honestly, I'm really not sure," I answered her. "Earlier, the weirdest thing happened. I was not able to remember any of my family. I couldn't remember my mother's name, my father's, or even my sibling's. I couldn't even remember what they looked like."

"Hmm! That is interesting. Have you ever thought that maybe because you lived in such a horrible place, your mind erased any memory of it to make room for better memories?" Sam asked me.

"Well...I'm unsure if that is the case here Sam, but what you are saying makes sense. Right now, all I can remember was living in a horrible town, leaving, and never looking back." I told her.

— 🫶 —

That night, I didn't get any sleep. Every time I closed my eyes, I saw this image of a woman beating me until I would spit blood out my mouth. Also, having that awful nightmare our first night in this house with the woman standing in my room. These dreams were starting to mess with me, so I decided to call Sam.

I didn't want Sam to get the wrong impression about me. We seem to be hitting it off pretty well. I could definitely see our friendship going in the right direction.

"Hey Sam! Sorry to call you so late; I just...I really needed someone to talk to. I'm having a hard time adjusting here. It's funny because I would have thought it would be the kids having the issue." I said as she answered the phone.

"No problem at all. What's going on?" she asked me.

As I began telling Sam about the dreams and inability to sleep, it was almost like I had a light bulb moment. Maybe deep down, I just needed to adjust to the the new place. Maybe my mind is just playing tricks on me. Just before hanging up with Sam, she recommended I see a doctor, and maybe they could refer me to a psychiatrist. She also stated she knew a good psychiatrist in town once I got my referral. She told me his name is Dr. Bryant. Apparently, she saw him a couple of times when she went through a very bad situation in her life with an ex-boyfriend of hers.

I hesitated to take her doctor's information, but I knew I could not bear another night like the last two nights, so I wrote his information down.

CHAPTER 8

The clock tower chimes. Its beautiful sound echoes through the entire town, and I glance down at my watch to notice that it's now 8 a.m. Once again, the clock tower was right on time to ensure that everyone was at work and school. I had already asked my boss if I could take some time off to visit the doctor that Sam had recommended.

My boss is a very nice and understanding man. He told me to take as much time as I needed and to not worry about coming in if it was getting too late.

The doctor's office wasn't that far from my house. The good thing about this town is it takes about 5-10 minutes to get anywhere around here. According to my GPS, it will take me exactly seven minutes to get there.

To reach Dr. Bryant's office, you have to take the scenic route through downtown. Downtown in Shelly Grove is a peaceful and serene place, very different from a busy city. There are no tall buildings or noisy traffic, just a calming and beautiful environment.

Following the turn-by-turn directions from the robotic lady who sounded like Siri, I couldn't help but notice something peculiar about this town. There was a distinct absence of cars and people. It was as if the town had taken a collective pause, a moment of stillness in the midst of life's constant motion.

"Odd," I say to myself.

Dr. Bryant's office is perched on Hill Street. As I parked my car and made my way to the door, I couldn't help but be captivated by the view. I turned, shielding my eyes from the bright sun, and there it was-Mrs. Sally's house, majestically crowning the top of the hill. The street, I realized, led all the way down to the bottom. It was a moment of revelation, a glimpse into the town's unique geography.

This is why they call it Hill Street.

The doctor's office is located in a building with several businesses, and Dr. Bryant's office is on the second floor. The building is so old, but luckily, it has an elevator, so I decided to take it to the second floor instead of the stairs.

As I entered the elevator, I was quickly reminded of how old this building really is. The carpet was slightly worn and emitted an unsettling stench. The elevator door made a creaking sound as it closed. Even though I was only going up a floor, I braced myself as the elevator began to ascend, unsure if I would make it alive from the way the elevator shook as it went up.

Coming off the elevator, I noticed his office sits directly in front of the elevator doors. So it was a straight shot to the door.

When I entered the office, it felt like a very welcoming environment. The windows were open, and you could see the view from outside. It was nice because you could also see the clock tower and how it sits in the middle of the town park.

As I approached the front desk, the receptionist greeted me with a smile, showing her pearly white teeth. She could definitely be on one of those Colgate commercials.

"Hello, are you here to check in?" she asks with a big smile, continuing to show her bright white teeth.

"Yes, I called a few days ago to schedule an appointment. My doctor gave me a referral to see a psychiatrist, and a friend recommended Dr. Bryant. She told me he was the best in town. Is he nice? Does he see a lot of patients? Sorry, I'm rambling." I say while fiddling with my fingers. "I tend to do that when I get nervous."

Laughing, she says, "You're fine. You have nothing to be nervous about. This is a safe space here, and Dr. Bryant has a great relationship with all his patients."

I really liked this receptionist. She didn't make you feel like you were there for mental issues. She talked with me as if we were friends. It felt good to meet another person in Shelly Grove with such a loving personality.

The receptionist reminded me so much of one

of those supermodels on the TV show Top Model with Tyra Banks. She was tall and super skinny, with the prettiest blond hair and brightest blue eyes. Her skin was perfect. It was almost as if she had been pulled out of a magazine and placed right here at the front desk.

As I waited in the lobby for the doctor to take me back, I noticed all the beautiful artwork hung on the walls. The tone of the music was just right; it almost felt like they were playing something by Beethoven. This place did make you feel comfortable, and this is what you need when you come to a place like this.

As I patiently waited, my eyes wandered and caught sight of a photograph that sparked a sense of familiarity within me. The image depicted a charming house perched atop a hill; it was captivating. The contrast between the darkness of the night and the warm illumination that sprung from the house was truly mesmerizing. Upon closer inspection, I was struck by the realization that the house in the photograph bore an uncanny resemblance to Mrs. Sally's home.

As I stared at the photo, I thought how

weird it is to have a picture of Mrs. Sally's house hanging on the wall of a psychiatrist's office. I couldn't help myself, so I asked the receptionist whose house was in the picture. For a minute, it was as if her world stopped when I asked her that question.

She looked at me, a little frightened. It was as if we were having a staring contest for a moment. She didn't blink, not once. Finally, she said, "Um, I'm not sure. A lot of the artwork came with the building."

Odd, I thought, but I was already there for one reason. I didn't need them to think I was even more crazy.

"Alice," a deep voice calls for me from the hallway beside the receptionist's desk. "Come on back." Finally, I can meet the doctor Sam spoke so highly of.

I quickly snapped to attention, taking my gaze off the receptionist's frightened expression.

Standing there a man who seemed to embody the image of a respected psychiatrist. He wore a white coat, a light blue button-up shirt, and a navy blue tie. I couldn't help but assume that this must be the famous Dr. Bryant, the one Sam had spoken so highly of.

"Hello," I say as I reach my hand out to shake his.

He instructs me to follow him to the back. Even though the receptionist told me I had nothing to worry about, I was still nervous. He didn't seem like the welcoming type, if you ask me. He didn't crack one smile. Aren't they supposed to make you feel good to be coming to a place like this? Maybe he needed to take notes from his receptionist.

I really hope this guy is nice.

"Take a seat," he says as he motions his hand towards the couch in what seems to be his office.

It was a cozy little office if you ask me. Once again, there was a lot of artwork hung on the walls. In the corner sat a cherry wood desk. His desk was neat—the complete opposite of the one I have at work.

His office was spotless. If I had a white glove and administered a dust check like they do in the military, I'm sure he would pass with flying colors.

"So, what brings you in today?" he asks while finally cracking a smile big enough for me to see that his teeth are equally as white as the receptionist's.

"Oh, thank goodness." *Wait, did I say that out loud?*

"What's wrong?" he asks.

"Sorry, I was nervous about coming here, and when you weren't smiling, I wasn't sure if I had made a good choice. But my friend said you were good, so I figured I'd give you a chance. But then you walked me into this office and still weren't smiling; I was certain I had made a mistake." I say. "I'm doing it again. Babbling."

"Alice, Alice," Dr. Bryant says, chuckling. "Calm down. I like to get to know my patients more personally when I get into my office. I'm one cool guy, you can believe that." he says while smiling.

Meeting with the doctor was great! He was nothing like I was expecting. I pictured him as an older man with gray hair and maybe some big bifocal glasses. To my surprise, he was the total opposite. He looked like he could be in his mid-thirties and wasn't wearing glasses at all. He had low-cut, silky, pitch-black hair and a goatee.

He was very nice and understanding. We went through the things I could remember about my hometown and the dreams I was having. He began to explain that I had dissociative amnesia.

"Amnesia? I thought that only happened when you got old or got in a terrible accident?" I ask.

He chuckled and explained, "Traumatic events can also cause amnesia. Sometimes our brains, when they have experienced something so treacherous, tend to push that in the back of our minds and replace it with things and events that make us happy."

"Hmm. Interesting." I say.

"How about we start you with a low dose of sleeping medicine? It's not the type of medication that will make you sleepy to where you feel drowsy the next day. We can try this for a few days, and if it works great for you, I'll put in a 90-day supply for you." He explains.

"Well, my friend recommended you, and she says you're good, so I need to trust that you are.

So I think I'll take the medication. I'm desperate, to be honest, and need to get some rest," I say.

"Great, let me write it up. Give me just a moment, and I'll be right back with your prescription." He explained as he stood up from his chair and left his office.

While I sat in the office waiting for him to return, I shook my head in disbelief. I couldn't believe I was talking to a psychiatrist. I don't think I've ever had to come to see a doctor like this before. At this point, I thought, *what a way to spend my first week in Shelly Grove.*

CHAPTER 9

———

I hadn't experienced a good night's sleep in a while. After speaking with the doctor and getting my prescription, I spent days looking at the bottle. I've never been the type of person who wanted to take medicine. I've always felt like it's a tiny thing that has a way of controlling your body.

In my situation, this pill is supposed to help me get some sleep, but who knows what it is doing to the inside of me.

These are all thoughts I have to overcome. I can't be afraid of getting help from this doctor. Sam recommended him at the end of the day, and if she says he's good, he must be. I need someone other than Mrs. Sally and Mr. Gerald to trust in this town, so why not start with Sam? After all, she comes from two of the sweetest people we have ever met.

I was startled by the sound of my doorbell, which let me know I must have fallen into a deep sleep unexpectedly.

I jumped out of bed to check the door to see who could possibly be visiting me so early on a Saturday. This brought back flashbacks of times I would be woken at different times of the night by a woman. She never cared what time of the night or day it was; she would just come when she felt it was convenient.

The clock tower chimed, echoing throughout the entire town.

Oh my goodness, it's Saturday morning. Does the clock tower chime on the weekends as well? I looked down at my watch, and it was 9 a.m.

I made it to the door, and what a pleasant surprise. It was sweet, Mrs. Sally. I was so happy to see her and wanted to thank her for telling me about her amazing daughter, Sam. I opened the door, and the weirdest thing happened. Mrs. Sally stepped into my house without even an invite, but then she recognized her flaw and stepped back out and asked politely if she could enter.

Surprised by her actions, I thought, *I know this lady did not just step into my house without me inviting her in.* But remembering how nice of a person Mrs. Sally is, I let it go and invited her in. I also need to remember that we're not in the South anymore. People may be different in Oklahoma.

Mrs. Sally greeted me with the biggest hug and told me how glad she was that I had met her daughter and that we were hitting it off. She told me she always wanted Sam to have a sister she could grow up with and become best friends with. I started to share with her the relationship I thought I had with a sister I thought I had, but I couldn't remember anything about her or even that I had a sister.

I was stunned. I couldn't get my thoughts together, and at this point, Mrs. Sally could see something was wrong with me. As a cover-up, I just said, "Well, you know what? She has one now."

Mrs. Sally's face lit up like a Christmas tree. She looked so happy to hear those words come out of my mouth—maybe a little too happy if you ask me—but she's so sweet; who could be mean to her?

After that very uncomfortable conversation with Mrs. Sally, I decided to show her around the house and let her see how we decorated it. I started with the kitchen because, in the South, the kitchen is the heart of the home. Mrs. Sally loved the colors and the southern farmhouse theme.

Next, I decided to show her the living room. She was amazed by the wall décor. I'm just glad I didn't have to worry about furniture. Finding a fully furnished home with furniture matching all your decorations is hard. It was the perfect place.

"It looks nice in here, but..." Mrs. Sally says with an expression on her face that tells me she doesn't like what I've done with the place. "Where is the rug I had lying on the floor?"

"Oh yes," I reply with a chuckle. "It was beautiful and fluffy too, but I don't care for rugs. I don't like how they hold smells."

"Is that right? Well, you didn't think to ask me if that was okay? Why change anything if the house came prepared for you child?" Her eyes widened, and from what I could see, it seemed like her eyes were getting a little darker at that moment.

"Um, I'm sorry I didn't see anything in the lease agreement that I couldn't change anything. It only mentioned that if I changed anything, I needed to make sure it was back to its original state if we moved out. I'm so sorry." I say with a sorrowful look on my face.

We stood there staring into each other's eyes for what felt like forever. She didn't say a word with her hands propped on her hips as if she was ready to blow a gasket.

Standing there waiting for her reply, I suddenly had what felt like a flashback. I was lying on the floor in a house with a fluffy rug that tickled my cheeks. It was so real; I could almost feel the rug touching my skin at that very moment. But for some reason, I can't remember anything past our airport trip.

"Did you hear me child?" Mrs. Sally says.

"I'm so sorry; what did you say?" I ask.

"Ugh!" Rolling her eyes. "I said don't worry

about the rug. I was overreacting. That was a special rug to me. It belonged to...well... it belonged to my mother, and I just wanted to keep it close."

Interesting. Why put a rug that belonged to your, I'm assuming, now-deceased mother in a rental property?

"You know what? I'm sorry, but I should have asked first. I can put it back down if it means that much to you." I didn't mean that. But deep down inside, I hoped she would say not to worry about it.

She studies my face and then bites down on her bottom lip. "It's okay. Don't you worry about it dear; I'm just overreacting. That thing was old anyway. I'll have Gerald come get it one of these days."

"Great, well, let me show you the kid's rooms. I think you'll love what they've done with them." I say as we walk towards the stairs.

"Wait!" she says loudly. Something mysteriously stopped her in her tracks. "Why are your drapes hung this way, and why did you choose this color? I don't think this matches that well."

Oh my goodness! What in the world is wrong with this woman? She is catching me off guard today. This isn't the sweet woman we had breakfast with on our first day here. I would have never expected this behavior from her.

Maybe it's because she's older. She could just be set in her ways.

"You know what, never mind. Sorry, I have my own way of doing things," she says, waving her hands at me, brushing off what she had said about the drapes.

As we ascended the stairs, I was eager to show her the kids' rooms. Our first stop was Adam's room. Standing in thoughtful silence, she carefully observed every corner of the room, her finger gently resting on her chin as she meticulously scanned the surroundings. *What on earth is she doing?* I thought.

"So what made him decorate it like this?" she asks. I look around, trying to wrap my head around what could be wrong with a little boy's decorations with all his favorite video game characters. He had Mario and Sonic posters plastered on the wall. He has a Minecraft comforter set on his bed and a Nintendo Switch hooked up to his TV.

"Do you always let him play that thing?" she asks, pointing her finger at his Nintendo Switch.

"Oh, no, no, no. He knows he can only play for two hours a day, and when school is in, he can only play once he's done with his homework." I explain.

She nodded slowly as if she didn't believe a word I was saying, "Right?"

Next, we checked out Kandice's room. I can't see anyone having an issue with her room. She had what I call a reader's room. She has a small bookshelf that is filled with books from different genres. Her room sits above the garage, and in the window, she has a nice bench that she sits on when reading her books.

"Now, this is my kind of room," Mrs. Sally grins.

"Right?" I respond. "The kids both have their own personalities. Kandice is quieter, whereas Adam is more outgoing and adventurous."

After our moment in the kids' rooms, we

finally decided the tour was over. Mrs. Sally informed me that she had to head out but would love to see more of the place another day. Making our way to the door, she mentioned the welcome party they hold for every new person who moves into the area.

She insisted on having this party for the kids and me and wouldn't take no for an answer. I was exhausted from the move, starting work, and getting the kids started at their new school. The last thing I wanted was a meet-and-greet with a bunch of people in town.

On the other hand, Mrs. Sally is such a sweet lady, it was impossible to let her down. It was all over her face how much she wanted this party to happen, and to tell her no would crush her heart. So, I put aside my feelings and told her we could have the party.

Mrs. Sally was ecstatic that I agreed to let her have the party. She instantly pulled out her phone and started going through her contact list. It was almost unreal how many people this lady knew. She talked about catering, champagne glasses, and tablecloths. She talked about how many guests would come and the theme for the party.

She was very persistent and wanted to make sure this was the party of the century. Those were literally the words that came out of her mouth. Whoever she was speaking with must have got an earful. Once she got off the phone, I say, "Mrs. Sally, it doesn't have to be this big of a party."

"Oh hush, child," she quickly replied. Her face went from smiling to immediately looking as if she was ready to rip me apart. "Don't you know how to appreciate when someone is doing a nice thing for you?" she asked.

I was very shocked to hear her say that to me. I barely know this lady, and she speaks to me this way. I was even more surprised by the look on her face. Once again, I swallowed my pride and said, "Um... thank you, I guess."

After speaking with Mrs. Sally, it was time for her to go. She had so much to start planning for this party. She started walking down the stairs on the porch. She pulled her fancy bag over her shoulders, put her sunglasses on, and put her hat on her head. She turned around, tipped her sunglasses, and said, "By the way child, this party will be next Saturday; I'll pick you up Friday to get you something nice to wear to your welcome party."

My jaw dropped, and I couldn't believe this woman could organize such a party in so little time.

Before stepping back into the house, I noticed something rather interesting. As she walked to her car, a woman stood across the street, staring at her with the most frightened look. Mrs. Sally glanced at her and gave her somewhat of a smile. She was a little creepy if you ask me.

There was something about this lady that I couldn't shake off. She was an older woman with salt and pepper-colored hair. She was wearing a pink sweater and Bermuda shorts.

Have I seen her before?

I shook my head to clear any weird thoughts of what I had witnessed. After closing the door, I leaned against it to gather my thoughts. "This woman is nuts," I say to myself, but she is Mrs. Sally, and the town loves her, so why not have this party?

CHAPTER 10

It's 6 p.m. on a Friday, and there goes the clock tower again. The first time I heard the chime, I thought the clock would only sound at the beginning of the day, but I was wrong. It chimes on the hour every hour. It's a good thing it's not an annoying sound.

I had made it home from work and made sure the kids had already had dinner. Mrs. Sally was outside waiting for me in her shiny dark blue Rolls-Royce. Taking a deep breath, I walked outside to greet her, and to my surprise, Sam jumped out of the car. My level of excitement went from zero to ten instantly.

"Sam, I had no idea you would be joining us!" I say to her in a high-pitched voice.

Sam explained, "Yes, my mother called

me when she left your house. She insisted I accompany you all to help you find the perfect dress for your party. Knowing the party would be for you, I couldn't turn down the invite."

At this point, it didn't matter what Mrs. Sally had up her sleeve for the day. As long as Sam was with us, I knew we would have a great time.

"Well come on ladies, the dress isn't going to find itself." Mrs. Sally says as she places the sunglasses on her face.

"Right, we should probably get going," Sam says as she gestures for me to get into the car.

Driving through the town of Shelly Grove, the view is captivating, but one thing I found very odd was the way people in the town stood outside on the lawns. They stood there watching us as we drove by. Their heads followed the car's direction, and not one person blinked.

"Did you see that?" I asked Mrs. Sally and Sam.

"See what?" Sam ask.

"Um... nothing," I say. I didn't want them to think I was crazy.

It made me wonder if what Kandice was

saying about her school happened. The way these people stood there watching her car go by, you would have thought she was the president of the United States. Mrs. Sally was undoubtedly a woman of mystery. With her mysterious dark sunglasses, she tipped her shades and looked at each person as she drove by. This was strange if you ask me.

Why were all the people standing there? Why did they have a blank look on their faces? It was almost as if each person was under some spell. When her car passed their house, they would move as if they had come out of the spell and returned to their homes. "That was weird," I murmured under my breath.

Something else strange occurred. At that moment, the same woman I saw standing across the street looking at Mrs. Sally was also standing outside. It looked like she was out for a walk, so now I know she lives in my neighborhood. Shelly Grove is a weird town, but the kids like it, so I must love it for them.

"So Alice, what type of dress do you think you'll want to wear to your party?" Sam asked, looking at me eagerly and waiting for my response.

"Um...I really don't know. Dressing up isn't my thing, you know. As long as it's comfortable, I guess it doesn't matter to me." I reply.

Mrs. Sally laughs, "Child please," she says. "It must be something to show off your Coca-Cola-shaped body, my dear."

"Well, I don't think that matters," I say, followed by a light chuckle.

"There will be so many eligible bachelors there," she stated.

Is this the lady who greeted me and my kids on our first day here? Who does she think she is telling me what I have to wear and who I have to meet? Enough is enough, so I had to tell her what was on my mind.

"Mrs. Sally, isn't this my party? Don't I get to decide what I want to wear and who I want to talk to?"

Sam slowly turned from the front seat with a fearful look and then glanced back at her mom, but Mrs. Sally didn't even acknowledge what I said.

As we arrived at the shopping center, I couldn't get out of that car fast enough. "This woman has some issues," I mumble.

Trying to take in all that had happened during the drive to the shopping center, I felt someone come behind me and wrap their arm around mine. Luckily, it was Sam. "I know my mom can be a bit much, but I promise she means well," she told me as we stood there waiting for Mrs. Sally to exit the car.

I smiled at Sam, and we walked towards all the fancy stores Mrs. Sally had brought us to. I thanked Sam for tagging along and for being such a good friend. This day couldn't get any worse as long as she was around.

CHAPTER 11

——

I was completely over this day. Dress shopping here, shoe shopping there, and trying on countless handbags. It took hours to find the perfect dress, and honestly, I wasn't wearing the right shoes for walking around all day. Mrs. Sally was determined to make sure I had nothing but the best.

Does she always treat the locals like this? I thought to myself. The money she spent on me was ridiculous. I don't make that much monthly to buy half the things she got for me.

I couldn't bear it any longer. I had to let her know this was too much, and it was time to go. I stormed over to Mrs. Sally; before I could say anything, she turned around with the most intimidating look. "Is there a problem?" she asked.

"Um—" To my surprise, I had no words. I couldn't express to her how I felt. To be honest, I think I may be a little afraid of her at this point. She is like that bully in school. When you see her coming down the hallway, you either look the other way to avoid eye contact or you run. I couldn't run and had already made eye contact with her, so the next best thing was to turn around and walk away.

The walk back to the car was incredibly uncomfortable. I couldn't stop thinking about the person Mrs. Sally really is. I just knew she had a good heart and was a good person. I don't think I've ever met a bully before, but if I had to imagine one, she would fit the description. Sam broke the ice and ended our silence, "So I'm excited for the party. I know you're going to look amazing in the dress we picked out."

As she looked at me smiling, it seemed as if she was more excited about this party than I was. *Why is it that everyone is so ecstatic about this party?* I couldn't say much, so I just smiled back at her.

"Yeah, me too," I lie.

Fiddling my thumbs, I couldn't hold back any longer, so I asked her, "Is your mom always this scary?"

Sam laughed and said, "My mom wouldn't hurt a fly." Coming from Sam, you would think I could believe that, but there's something about her mom that doesn't convince me she is as innocent as Sam thinks she is.

We finally made it back to my house, and I couldn't wait to get away from Mrs. Sally. There's something about that woman that disturbs me. Adam and Kandice were overjoyed to see her. They both rushed out of the house to greet her. If only they had seen her today, I know they would have had a different impression of her.

Kids are like a pack of wolves; they can sniff out fear. I couldn't give them any indication that something was bothering me, so as a good mother, I told them to hug Mrs. Sally and Sam and say goodnight. Thanking them both for a great outing, I also wished them a good night and closed the door.

That night, even with the pills the doctor gave me, I found it very hard to sleep. I tossed and turned, unable to stop thinking about Mrs. Sally's smile and the shivers that ran through my body when she looked at me. There's something genuinely unsettling about her. I couldn't shake the image of how she tipped her sunglasses as if she were the ruler of the town and its people were her puppets. Her confidence is almost intimidating.

I couldn't stop thinking about the look Sam gave me in the car when I stood up to her mother. It was almost as if she was afraid of the response her mom would give me right after. I couldn't stop thinking about the people and how they were all standing outside as we drove by; it almost looked like they were in some trance.

Lastly, I couldn't stop thinking about this woman who had popped up twice. She looked frightened whenever Mrs. Sally was around. Something weird is up with this lady, and I need to figure it out if we're going to continue living in her house.

CHAPTER 12

—

After a sleepless night, I knew it was my big day for this party Mrs. Sally had arranged for me. Lying in bed and looking at the ceiling, I had another flashback. This time, I was arguing with a lady. I could see clearly how fearful I was of her. This flashback almost felt so real. It was the same fear I felt when speaking with Mrs. Sally.

Tears began to flow down my cheeks as if what I just experienced was something from my past.

"Get it together Alice," I said to myself.

I dread going to this party tonight, but I desperately need to figure this woman out. My poor friend Sam has no idea, but I'm almost convinced her mom is wicked or very crazy. Either way, I know I must be at this party tonight if I'm going to figure Mrs. Sally out.

The kids came running into my room with so much excitement. Adam said, "Mommy, are you ready to look like a princess tonight?" Concern was all I felt at that moment. I knew Mrs. Sally had put her spell on my kids. They love her and don't even know something is tremendously wrong with her.

"Mom, I know in the beginning I was a little hesitant about the kids at school, but I just want to say thank you. Thank you for moving us to this amazing town. I'm so glad we've met good people like Mrs. Sally, Mr. Gerald, and Sam," Kandice expressed to me while lying across the foot of my bed in her purple leggings and graphic T-shirt.

I didn't mention this before, but Adam and Kandice have no memory of their grandparents either. They don't even recall ever having grandparents. For their age, I could see how they would think that. As an adult, I know for a fact I wouldn't exist if they didn't have grandparents.

The kids have often told me they wish they had grandparents like Mrs. Sally and Mr. Gerald.

What do I say to that? Every now and then, I would ask them little questions like, "Have you two seen a photo book lying around here with pictures from our previous town?" I have also asked, "Do you all know where my photos of your grandmother are?" But they would always give me the same blank look and then shrug their shoulders.

Even though we have no memory of our past, maybe that is for the best. Maybe it's like Dr. Bryant said. Maybe my past was so traumatizing that my mind has finally let go of those memories. Maybe this town is the start of a new future for us.

I smiled at them, kissed their foreheads, and told them we had a big day ahead of us. This is what good parents do; we sacrifice our feelings to ensure our kids are happy. It doesn't matter that Mrs. Sally puts on like she is perfect because, in reality, she is the devil on the inside. I couldn't tell them what I felt; it would crush their little hearts.

"Come on you two. Let's head downstairs so I can make you two some breakfast," I say, trying to seem as if nothing is bothering me.

As I've mentioned, kids are like wolves—especially my kids. They could tell something was bothering me. It didn't matter that I was trying to brush it off by making them something to eat—they could still see it in my eyes.

"Mom, are you scared you'll meet like a boyfriend or something at the party?" Adam asked, grinning.

"What?" I couldn't believe my child just asked me that.

"Adam, shut up; Mom is not thinking about that kind of stuff." Kandice looks at me and winks.

"Well, all my friends at school talk about having boyfriends and girlfriends. How come mom can't have one?" Adam pleads my case.

Laughing at the two of them, I look at Adam and say, "Sweetheart, Kandice is right. I'm not thinking about that stuff right now."

"Well, I think you should, Mom. I'd like to have another guy around here to beat in Mario Kart. Besides, I'm out-ranked here. All you and Kandice talk about is girl stuff." Adam explains.

"We are not having this conversation!" I

chuckle as I push the two of them out of my bed. Come on, let's get downstairs to get—"

"Seriously though, Mom, what is bothering you?" Kandice asks with a serious face.

I can't tell them the truth about how I'm feeling. Mrs. Sally has done so much for us; I know the kids will only see it that way. Besides, they are only kids; they would never understand.

CHAPTER 13

—

Before the party tonight, I wanted to see my doctor to talk to him about the flashbacks and how real they felt. He agreed to see me today, so I quickly gathered my things. "Kids, I'll be back!" I yelled just as I was walking out the door.

The clock tower echoes. The sound resonated throughout the entire town.

The clock tower has now reminded me it's noon. I didn't want to spend too much time at Dr. Bryant's office, so I quickly navigated through traffic to meet him.

As I approached the doctor's office, I saw something quite interesting. *That car looks very familiar. What the—?*

It was Mrs. Sally walking out of his office. She was wearing her usual mysterious sunglasses and a dress that complimented her curves. It was weird seeing her at a psychiatrist's office. *I wonder what that's all about.*

Maybe this is the bad feeling I'm getting about her. Perhaps she really is crazy. But then again, I'm seeing the same doctor, so does that make me crazy, too?

Before I could continue my internal debate, I quickly jumped out of my car and crossed the street. I wasn't sure what my next move was, but all I knew was my feet were moving faster than I could think.

If I had taken a second, I could have come up with something to say to her, but the first thing that came out of my mouth once I approached her was, "I didn't know you knew the Psychiatrist here."

With a snobbish look, she said, "Honey, I know everyone in this town." She put on her sunglasses and walked away.

I'm so frustrated. This woman is literally everywhere. But I can't show how she's starting to get to me. There is something about her, and I need to get down to the bottom of it.

Shaking off my encounter with Mrs. Sally, I made a beeline toward the office building and swung open the door. I didn't realize how frustrated I was. I swung the door open so fast that I almost hit a lady.

The receptionist has always been kind to me when visiting my doctor's office. She makes a person feel so welcome in a place like this. I was so eager to see her, especially after seeing Mrs. Sally. I needed to see a friendly face before my doctor's visit. But to my surprise, she wasn't there. Shockingly, my doctor was the one who greeted me today.

"Come on back," he said.

As I sat in his office, there was an awkward moment of silence. For a doctor, aren't they supposed to start the visit with many questions? At least he could have asked me why I was there, but nothing came out of his mouth. He just stared at me.

To break the ice, I asked, "So, where is the receptionist?"

"Oh, she has the weekend off." He says casually.

"Oh, that's nice," I say, lowering my eyes.

"But don't worry, you will see her tonight at the party." He explains.

"Oh, okay, that's nice," I reply. "Wait, what? The party, are you serious?" I couldn't hold back any longer.

"Yeah, the party?" he says as if questioning my curiosity.

"Why is your receptionist attending my party?" I asked while gazing into his eyes, but he couldn't give me an answer. He just stared at me with a blank expression.

I'm so glad there was a couch in his office. All I could do was lay back and look up at the ceiling. This is getting a little ridiculous. I'm not getting married, nor am I this woman's child. Someone has to stop this mess.

With plenty of questions running through my head, the one that stuck out the most was the picture he had hanging in the lobby of what seemed to be Mrs. Sally's house. So, I asked my doctor about his artwork hanging in the lobby. He was open to sharing what each piece meant to him and why it was there. This was my time to ask him about the picture of Mrs. Sally's house.

He took a deep breath and responded to me, "Well... Mrs. Sally owns all the real estate in this town, so she wants a picture of her house to hang on all the walls of all her properties." It was almost as if he had to think of a reason it was out there in the first place. "By the way, it's an extremely lovely photo, so why not have it up?" Dr. Bryant asked.

"I see. Well, it is a lovely house. I can see why she would want to showcase it," I mutter under my breath. What he said was interesting because the receptionist seemed to think the picture came with the building.

After visiting my doctor's office, I had a lot of questions. Why would everyone come to my welcome party? I think I can understand the excuse he gave me about the photo, but my gut tells me something isn't right about this, and I really don't believe she's just handing out pictures of her house like it's Halloween candy.

I don't even know anyone here. It felt really strange knowing several people from town would be at this party tonight. With confusion all over my face and millions of thoughts running through my head, the only place that felt right to go was the donut shop where Sam worked.

Luckily, her shop wasn't very far from my doctor, so I decided to walk to see Sam to clear my head. She was the only person in this town I felt comfortable with.

CHAPTER 14

——

As I approached Sam's donut shop, I peeked in the window to ensure she wasn't slammed with customers. I saw her standing at the counter, engaged in a book. I wondered what she could be reading that had her attention.

"Hey, Sam! I was in the area and wanted to stop by and talk to you for a second before I go home to get ready for the party." I said as I entered the donut shop.

Surprised to see me, she immediately put the book away. "Oh, hey Alice! I wasn't expecting to see you until tonight," she said in a high-pitched tone

"What were you reading? It must have been very interesting for you to be so focused on the pages."

Sam chuckles and says, "Oh, it was nothing. It was just a book I found in my parents' house. It wasn't that good; I needed something to distract me. As you can see, we aren't that busy today. Everyone is probably getting ready for your party this evening. What did you need to talk to me about?"

"Well... this town is so beautiful, and I love how the people are super friendly. To me, something is a little off, though. Why is everyone coming to my party tonight? Why is your mom insisting I meet so many people in this town? Shouldn't that be up to me?" I expressed to Sam.

"Oh yes, I'm so sorry Alice, that you feel this way. Please let me explain. Let's have a seat. My feet are killing me anyway. I've been on them all day," she says, instructing me to this small round table.

I nodded and quickly sat at the table, eagerly waiting to hear what she had to say.

"So I know my mom can be a bit much, but she means well, I promise. Believe it or not, she does this for all the newcomers. She has such a big heart," she explains.

"Really, how? Why? I mean, how can she afford that?" My level of curiosity is now at an all-time high.

Laughing, Sam continues explaining. "My parents, let's just say, are very wealthy people. I mean, they own all the real estate here in Shelly Grove. She's always wanted to do more with her wealth."

Interesting.

"So you see, my mom built a close community where everyone got along. Almost like family, you know. My mom has always been one to love family. She's always wanted a big family. But unfortunately, they only had one child." Sam explains as she lowers her gaze and fiddles with her fingers.

"Why didn't they have more children?" I asked out of curiosity.

"My mom wasn't able to have children anymore, and for a while, it tore her and my dad apart. I almost thought they would get a divorce, but they are strong, so they stuck it out and found other ways to have a family. Like building up this community." She explains while rubbing her eyes, almost as if trying to hold back a few tears.

I placed my hand over my mouth, "Oh my goodness, Sam, I'm so sorry. I had no idea. I couldn't imagine going through that."

"Hey, it's okay. We have learned to live with it, but this is why she is so passionate about tonight's party. She wants you and the kids to fit into this community just like everyone else," she explains, grabbing my hands and giving them a light squeeze.

A tear or two may have crept out and fallen down my cheeks. This was so sad, and I felt terrible for Mrs. Sally.

"Please don't feel bad, Alice. My parents are fine now, but if this makes you feel any better, no one has left this town since she rebuilt it. People love her here, and they love the family feel this community brings," she explains as she tilts her head slightly and smiles without showing her teeth.

"I get it now. Thank you so much." Still holding Sam's hands, I also give her hands a light squeeze.

It was the right decision to come and speak

with Sam. She made me feel so much better and even opened my eyes a little more to who Mrs. Sally is. I can see why her mom wanted us to become friends. Sam is the best.

I felt like a horrible person, thinking her mom could be the devil on the inside. No wonder my kids have fallen in love with her so much. All she wants is a place of peace. I mean, isn't that what we all want? This world is full of so much corruption; why not live in a community filled with happiness?

CHAPTER 15

—

After speaking with Sam, I knew there was only one last thing to do. I needed to hurry home so I could get ready for this party. I had stalled long enough and needed to get ready.

While driving back to my house, I felt remorseful for Mrs. Sally and Mr. Gerald. I can't imagine being in their shoes and being told I'd never be able to have kids again. Poor Mr. Gerald. I can only imagine how he felt. He probably wanted a son with whom he could play catch outside in the yard.

I'm a horrible person thinking Mrs. Sally was the devil.

Maybe that's why they wanted to feed us the first day we moved here. Maybe they saw my kids, and it made them happy in some way. Maybe this is why she wanted me to get close to Sam.

I'm such an idiot.

I needed to find a way to make this up to Mrs. Sally. If I had the time, I would head to her house and give her the biggest hug. I want her to know badly how sorry I am, even though she doesn't know I thought she was the devil.

I quickly pulled into my driveway, dashed out of the car, and slammed the door behind me. I ran up the porch steps, skipping every other step, until I reached my front door. I swung it open to express my excitement about tonight's party to the kids.

I really should stop doing that. I mean, I almost hit a lady today swinging the door open.

"KIDS COME DOWNSTAIRS!" I screamed as I entered through the front door.

I could hear both sets of footsteps running through the hallway upstairs and finally making it down the stairs. "Mom, what is wrong with you?" Kandice asked.

"Have you been smoking?" Adam also asked.

"Nope," I say with a smile on my face.

"Have you been drinking? I mean, you have

been gone pretty long. I almost didn't think we were going to this party tonight." Adam explains.

"No honey, I haven't been drinking or smoking or any other preposterous ideas you have bunched in that head of yours," I reply.

"So what's wrong with you then? Why did you come in the house screaming for us to come downstairs?" Kandice asked, looking a bit confused.

Once again, I couldn't tell them I thought Mrs. Sally was the devil. I also think my conversation with Sam was a little too deep to share with two kids. So I smiled at them and hugged them tight.

"Mom, you're squeezing my brains out," Adam mumbles. "I can barely breathe."

"Sorry baby, I just felt the need to hug you two. I love you two so much and can't imagine my life without you." I explain while planting a soft kiss on both their foreheads.

Standing there holding the two of them, I could picture it now: Mrs. Sally sitting on a doctor's table while Mr. Gerald was sitting on the uncomfortable chairs they have in the exam rooms, leaning over and gripping his wife's hand. They were probably eagerly waiting for some doctor to come in and tell them they were a certain number of months pregnant.

I could also picture the doctor standing in front of the closed door with his head down, trying to prepare himself for what he was about to say. He probably had his cream-colored folder tucked underneath his armpit and was tugging at his white physician coat with his other hand. I could imagine him being extremely nervous at that moment as he lifted his head and, with hesitation, extended his hand out to turn the doorknob.

I could picture the doctor entering the exam room and Mrs. Sally and Mr. Gerald lifting their gaze at the provider, eagerly awaiting the good news, but soon to only find out that they are no longer able to produce children.

Sadly, I could picture the provider delivering the bad news to them both. Mrs. Sally would then lift her hands to cover her face as she screamed and cried because the family she desperately longed for was now only going to be a dream for her.

At that moment, I could also see Mr. Gerald rubbing his wife's back with the palm of his hand, trying to keep her calm while holding back his own tears to remain strong for her. This day was probably the worst day of their lives.

I felt sympathy at that moment, trying to imagine that day as if I were a fly on the wall and could see how this doctor's visit went for them. Tears began to creep down my cheeks and landed on Adam's curly black hair. Luckily, it was thick enough that he couldn't feel my tears dripping in his hair.

Sniffling, I continued to hug the kids.

"Are... you okay, mommy?" Adam asked as he lifted his head from my bear hug.

"I'm fine baby; I just needed to hug you two before we started doing anything else," I reply.

"All right Mom, enough of this sobby... stuff," Adam says while clapping his hands together.

Laughing at the fact that my little boy is not a baby anymore and doesn't want too much mommy love, I say, "Don't we have a party to get ready for?"

Kandice immediately looked up at me and had the biggest smile on her face.

"Mom, I've always wanted to do this. I've been watching these TikToks on how to do makeup and trust me, I'm going to make you look so good," she says.

First off, I had no idea my own daughter liked to watch TikTok. Every time I see her, she is buried in a book, but I guess that's the world we live in now. Social media has taken over and is now the cookbook or, in Kandice's case, the new makeup tutorial magazine.

Quickly running up the stairs, I could hear her scrambling around in the drawers. She was probably trying to find my curling iron and makeup brushes. She was determined that I was attending this party looking oh-so flawless tonight.

Why not let her give it her all so I could look my best tonight?

If I'm being honest with myself, I was also very eager to get to this party. I wanted to apologize to Mrs. Sally for seeming so ungrateful. I felt terrible for how I acted when she offered to take me shopping.

I desperately needed her to see how thankful I was for all the nice things she tried to do for me and the kids. She wasn't the devil, but a sweet person trying to make me and the kids feel welcome in this town. I had to put aside my pride and make things right. By the way, I can't be the only person in Shelly Grove who hates this lady. Everyone here loves her and talks so highly of her.

CHAPTER 16

—

The clock tower chimes, and it's now 7 p.m. How ironic is that? I felt like Cinderella at this moment trying to make it to the ball, but this Cinderella has kids, and at this moment, she is trying to rush them out of the house. There is no way I can be late. "Kids, come on, lets go!" I yell as I rush out the door, holding up my dress so it won't drag on the ground.

Running for the car, Adam dives into the front seat, and Kandice pulls up her dress so it doesn't get stuck in the door. Both of them are out of breath from racing to the car.

"You ready Mom? Let's get going. We can't be late for the party," Kandice says while checking her lip gloss in the tiny mirror, which she has stashed in her wristlet.

"Please, it's called fashionably late Kandice. We have got to give the people something to look at when we walk through the door. I mean, we clean up nice, don't you think?" Adams says while tugging at his jacket.

Laughing at the two of them, I hit the gas, and we headed for the hill.

— 🐻 —

Shelly Grove is a beautiful town. Even at night, the lights are lit up throughout the town. Driving to Mrs. Sally's house always gives the best view of the town. I can see why she decided to move up here. You can see all the lights and all the houses looking down from her home.

As she said, everyone from town was coming to my party tonight. Not one light was on in the houses in town, and not one car was in the driveway. Everyone was going to be here, and I was very happy to officially meet my neighbors.

Pulling into her driveway, I felt like royalty. A lovely man was standing outside in a tuxedo and white gloves. As the kids and I approached the front door, he greeted us at my window and said he would gladly park my car for me. As the kids and I exited the car, the nice man grabbed my hand to ensure I wouldn't trip.

Mrs. Sally has outdone herself.

Imagine my surprise when I saw a red carpet leading into her house. It was a sign that tonight's party would be a unique experience for me and my children. We had never received this kind of attention before.

As we were about to enter, a gentleman in a striking all-black tuxedo, complete with a black cummerbund, a white button-up dress shirt, and a black bowtie, rushed out. He was even wearing white gloves. He informed me that I couldn't step onto the red carpet without an escort, and then he reached out his hand to guide me onto the red carpet.

This was it for me. I threw in the towel; Mrs. Sally had officially won me over.

Upon entering her house, I felt like I was stepping into a ballroom. There was a chandelier hanging and lights twinkling everywhere. Women were dressed in gowns, and men wore tuxedos. The lighting was perfect, and the music was just right. It was the most elegant party I had ever attended.

We were greeted by a waiter holding a platter with several champagne glasses. I looked at Adam and Kandice and saw the sparkle in their eyes. I love Mrs. Sally even more for this experience. She has truly made my kid's day. This will be a day they will never forget.

Sam spotted me and ran over to greet us. "You guys look so amazing," she said. I also complimented her gown. I had never seen her in red before, but tonight, she wore a red sequin gown with white gloves that went up her arms.

"Your mom outdid herself with this party. I feel like I'm on an episode of Bridgerton in one of the ball scenes. The only thing missing is my prince charming trying to woo me to marry him." I say with a chuckle.

Sam began showing us around and introducing us to several people who live in our neighborhood. Everyone seemed to love the gown Mrs. Sally and Sam helped me pick out.

A lady was kind enough to say, "Girl, you look so good in teal." Another guest was fascinated by how my gown flared like a mermaid's tail and hugged my curves.

Chuckling, Sam says, "Don't break no hearts tonight with that dress friend."

Laughing at her, "Girl, you are so funny. I'm just kind of glad I went through with this. I've never gotten this dressed up before."

"Mom, I see Chris and John from school," Adam's eyes widen. "Can I go say hi to them?"

"Oh yes, I also see Jenny and Ashley. Can I go speak to my friends as well?" Kandice also asks.

It didn't take my kids long to decide they didn't want to spend the whole night with their mommy. This shouldn't surprise me; they will get older one day, and mommy will be their last priority. However, who would I be to tell them no? "Sure, go ahead."

Smiling at the kids as they ran off to be with their friends reassures me that we have found a place we can now call home. A mother couldn't be happier.

Kandice has finally stopped feeling tense about school and has started opening up to some of the girls in her class. She has even asked to have a sleepover or two, but I wanted to get our house in order before agreeing to the sleepovers. I can tell she has some good friends; they planned to wear purple tonight just because that was Kandice's favorite color.

I watched as she approached her friends. They complimented her on her light purple gown, which was also covered in sequins. Adam seemed to fulfill his desire to become the most popular kid in school. When all the boys from his school saw him, they were immediately impressed with his shiny black and blue tuxedo jacket and flashy black and blue dress shoes.

"Are you going to stand here all night smiling at the kids, or are you ready to meet some of the hotties around town?" Sam asks as she grabs my arm, interrupting my deep thoughts.

"Those are my babies, but I guess I'm ready to see what Shelly Grove has to offer," I say with a chuckle.

Sam is so sweet; she is destined to find me love. I almost felt like a candidate for one of those dating shows. *What's it called? Oh, yes, the Bachelorette.*

"Girl, it's time for you to get out of your

comfort zone and meet some of these fine men we have here. Just because I'm single doesn't mean you have to be." Sam reminds me.

I'm so glad I met this silly friend of mine. She really does make this place feel like home.

"Do I need to put on a name tag for the guys you have lined up for me?" I ask with a chuckle.

"Hey, if you like it, I love it," she replies.

I chuckled at her comment but also thanked her for the kind gesture. "Thank you, but I'm not sure I'm ready to talk to anyone right now. I mean, I have a lot going on. The kids and I have just started to get settled in, and I'm now able to have a full eight hours of sleep."

Sam would not take no for an answer. I can see where she got it from. Mrs. Sally is the same way.

Since I was dressed up in this really expensive dress that compliments every curve on my body, why not engage in conversation with a nice guy? Why not let someone tell me how beautiful I'm looking tonight? It's not every day that I hear those words anyway. So I took Sam up on her offer, and we began to scan the room.

Finally, I noticed a guy staring at me as if I were the only person standing in the room. He had the loveliest smile and the kindest eyes. Sam observed our eye contact, so she waved him over. I was extremely nervous. I hadn't talked to a guy since Adam and Kandice's dad.

What was his name again?

As he got closer to us, my heart began to pound. What do I say to a guy like that? His tux was well put together, and his watch looked more expensive than anything I own. *Would he even want to talk to a woman like me?* I thought.

This was it; he was finally standing right before me, and with no words in mind, all I could say was, "So how do you like the party?"

He chuckled and said, "I'm not sure it hasn't even started yet."

I felt silly at that moment. "Duh, Alice. You did just get here." I mutter under my breath.

I just knew that was the beginning and the end of our conversation. A man who looks like that doesn't want to talk to someone who says stupid things like I did. To my surprise, he wanted to continue with our conversation. So he introduced himself and told me his name was David. He also told me he worked for the police department here in town.

Man, he's good-looking, can dress, and holds a gun. *This guy is someone I'd be interested in.* But I had to pull myself together and stay calm. I had just met the guy, and who knows, he could be cute on the outside but a terrible person on the inside.

I know I just got to the party, but it felt like I had been talking to this guy for hours. We exchanged numbers and talked about possibly having dinner someday. As we continued our conversation, there was a sudden chime. That chime sounded familiar. Then, it was like a light bulb came on in my head. It was almost identical to the chime the clock tower gives out.

It was fascinating how everyone, including the servers, immediately stopped what they were doing and looked up at the staircase. Even weirder, the guy I was talking to reacted in the same way as everyone else. He quickly looked away from me and stared at the stairs like everyone else.

The mystery was over, and I could hear a sweet voice from the speakers. The voice said, "Welcome everyone. Thank you for attending the welcome party for Alice and her two children, Adam and Kandice." It was clear to me that the voice coming from the speaker was Mrs. Sally's, but where on earth was she?

Suddenly, you see her walking down the staircase in this astonishing gown. She is covered in gold. Her gown is covered in gold sequins, and it has a freaking cape. It complimented her hourglass figure. *Man, she looks amazing at her age.* Also, she is wearing gold heels to complement her dress. She is wearing the same gloves that went up her arms like Sam. Additionally, she has gold jewels in her hair and gold shimmer all over her shoulders. She looks breathtaking.

This was like a real-life fairytale, and I was the princess, and Mrs. Sally was the queen. At this point, I looked past all these people being extremely weird and focused on how beautiful she looked. No wonder the people were so fixated on her. She had the best dress in the whole town. I honestly don't think she bought it from any of the dress shops here in Shelly Grove.

Mrs. Sally walked up to me and greeted me with a kiss on my cheek and a warm hug. "I'm so glad you are here," she whispered in my ear. *A little weird,* I thought to myself, but I guess this is who she is. At least, that was the excuse I gave.

I wasn't sure if she knew the guy I was talking to, so I introduced her to him. Weird enough, he grabbed her hand, planted the softest kiss on her hand, and said, "It's always a pleasure to see you, Mrs. Sally." It was clear that everyone loved her, but my goodness, even my mystery guy also loved her.

Standing there patiently waiting for David to release her hand, I noticed something rather... well, rather strange. Everyone stared at us until Mrs. Sally announced it was time to eat. Then, oddly enough, everyone quickly went about their night like normal. It almost reminded me of the day we were driving by. *But again, her dress is breathtaking. Who wouldn't want to stare at her? Right?*

CHAPTER 17

───

As we approached the dining area, I was surprised at the sight before me. I've seen this in many movies, but nothing like this in real life. Do people really live this way? I mean, is this what life was like for Sam growing up? *My goodness, how loaded is Sam's family?* I thought to myself.

I was amazed by the red carpet, but what took me by surprise was when several waiters emerged and stood in front of tables with silver platters. As they lifted the covers, I couldn't believe my eyes – the food looked like something from a magazine. I had to pinch myself. Was I dreaming? Am I really at a party of such high class?

My eyes widened in amazement at the

display of food she had. I understand Sam telling me why she does this party, but this seemed a bit much for me. Mrs. Sally made sure this night was all about me and the kids. She ensured we got the first pick at the food. As we walked up to the tables, everyone looked at us like we were the royal family. It was a little uncomfortable if you asked me.

People even offered to make our plates. I had one person try to pour me a drink. I'm not used to this type of treatment. I looked over at my kids; of course, Adam was eating this up. He loves this stuff. I even saw him snap his fingers at one of the servers.

Once we got our food, I spotted a small table away from the crowd. In an attempt to sit alone, Mr. Crammer, my boss of all the people, popped up out of nowhere. It didn't surprise me that he was dressed to impress. He was wearing an all-black tuxedo. The jacket was covered in black rhinestones. He wore a black brim fedora hat with a feather on the side and some black suede dress shoes. He assured me I had a spot already reserved at the main table.

"Mr. Crammer, what on earth are you doing here?" I asked him.

Staring at me, looking me up and down as if he was judging what I was wearing, my boss finally said, "Did you forget everyone in town is coming to this event tonight? Besides, you are my newest employee. Even if the most famous person came into town, I wouldn't miss this party."

"Oh yes, that's right. I keep forgetting that. Well... I'm glad you came," I said as he escorted me to the main table. As we walked next to each other, all I could think of was how he looked at me and how weird it was. It made me feel a little uncomfortable. Was he judging what I was wearing? Does he think I look hideous? Oh God, what if he was looking at me the same way David was? *I can't think about this; he's my boss, for goodness sake. Just stop thinking at all, Alice.*

I had to keep reminding myself of what Sam told me about her mom. I had to remember that Mrs. Sally is a sweet person and that she has a reason behind all of this. I had to put aside my feelings and smile for this lovely party she put together.

Despite what happened a few seconds ago and how my boss looked at me, he was being a gentleman. Once we reached the main table, he pulled mine and Kandice's chairs out so we could be seated. "Well, thank you, Mr. Crammer," I said to him. He looked at me, winked, and gave me a sweet smile.

I've noticed that I have this issue with forming my own opinion about people. Maybe I was overthinking it when I thought he was judging my gown. I mean, honestly, I really can't blame him. Look at what he's wearing. He looks like he's ready to walk down the red carpet, and I'm not talking about the one Mrs. Sally has out front.

I witnessed firsthand the positive traits my colleagues mentioned about him. He is genuinely an excellent boss. Observing his professional demeanor in the office was delightful, and even more rewarding to see his personal side outside of work.

After taking our seats, I was on cloud nine. Everything was nice. The food looked amazing, and we were all dressed up—something we had never done before. Nothing was going to take this smile away from me.

Wait a minute. Why isn't anyone eating? Why is everyone staring at me and the kids? I thought.

"Um... is something wrong. Did we grab the wrong set of silverware or something?" I asked one of the guests from the party. She looked at me with a creepy smile and said, "We don't eat until you take the first bite, dear."

No way. This can't be right.

Looking around the table, I was a little taken aback by the fact that no one was eating. I thought maybe that lady was joking when she said that, but she was right. No one picked up a fork or a spoon until I took the first bite.

This was a peculiar experience. I couldn't help but wonder if this is what it feels like to be a queen or a princess. Do they usually eat first before anyone else can? The thought lingered in my mind, making me feel a strange mix of curiosity and self-reflection.

The situation was becoming overwhelming, and I needed a moment to collect myself. I excused myself and set off in search of a bathroom. Mrs.

Sally and Mr. Gerald's house has many rooms, and I found myself navigating through countless doors before stumbling upon a bathroom at the end of the hall. The question echoed in my mind: *why would two people need a house with so many rooms?*

As I entered the bathroom, it was breathtaking. It smelled like roses, and she had a chandelier hanging from the ceiling. She even had those little fancy chocolates you get from a department store sitting on a crystal plate on the sink. If this were any other bathroom, I would pass on the candy, but this wasn't any other bathroom.

The sink had one of those LED mirrors, and the wallpaper looked like something from a European castle. For a guest bathroom, it was bigger than one of my kids' bedrooms.

After admiring the bathroom, I finally decided to check out my makeup. I never got the chance to look at it before we left the house, but I trust Kandice; I know she did an excellent job.

While admiring her work, I suddenly heard someone crying. I peeked out the door, and it was Sam. I started to walk out of the bathroom to ensure she was okay, but then I saw my boss, Mr. Crammer, walk up to her. My first instinct was to shut the door.

I've never seen Mr. Crammer talking to Sam; she has never mentioned anything about him. "So why would he, of all people, be coming to comfort Sam?" I asked myself. I cracked the door open to check on Sam and see what this was about. Did Sam have a secret lover she wasn't telling anyone about?

While peeking out the bathroom door, I noticed it was nowhere near what I thought it could have been. It was the very opposite if you ask me. Mr. Crammer and Sam were having what looked like a heated conversation. I could tell they didn't want to cause a scene, so they stood alone, whispering in a corner. You could see the tension between the two of them.

As I continued to spy on them, Mrs. Sally came out of nowhere, grabbed Sam's face, and shoved something in her mouth. From my standing angle, I couldn't see what she put in her mouth.

I couldn't sit there and watch anymore. Dashing out of the bathroom, I immediately ran over to them to see what was going on. "What in the world are you doing to her? Sam, are you okay?" I asked.

Sam looked over at me with tears running down her face. She immediately wiped her tears and gathered herself. She then said, "Come on Alice. You have a party to attend and many people to see you in this gorgeous dress." As we walked off, I looked over my shoulder and noticed the very angry look on Mrs. Sally and Mr. Crammer's faces.

As the night went on, so many thoughts raced through my mind. Why on earth would someone who spoke so highly of their daughter treat her like that? Why was my boss so angry with Sam? What on earth did Mrs. Sally put in Sam's mouth? Why is Sam acting as if nothing just happened?

Standing in disbelief, holding a glass of champagne, I looked at Sam. She was dancing and happy, and I couldn't understand what was happening. I looked at Mrs. Sally, and she was engaged in conversation with some of the people in the town. I looked over at my boss, and he was conversing with a waiter.

Each of them was in their own world doing their own things, but they were still hiding something. My suspicion about Mrs. Sally instantly returned, and I couldn't sit back and let this continue. I chugged my champagne and slammed it on the table beside me.

The suspense was killing me, and I had to get to the bottom of this. Assuring no one saw, I snuck away and started checking Mrs. Sally's several rooms. This lady has way too many rooms for her not to have secrets hidden in one of them.

Each room had a nicely made bed and perfect drapes hanging. Mrs. Sally is a woman with many secrets, and I can see that very well at this point. There must be something in this house that will give me some answers about who this lady really is.

Think Alice.

Finally returning to the hallway where this all started, I noticed a room at the end near the bathroom I was in. My curiosity started kicking in, and that gut feeling became more robust; I needed to check that room.

Creeping towards the door, a wave of fear washed over me, intensifying with each step. I cautiously placed my hand on the knob, my heart pounding in my chest, and glanced over my shoulder to ensure I was alone. With bated breath, I began to turn the knob, the sound echoing in the silence, my fear mounting with each click.

As the door began to open, I felt the firm grip of someone's hand wrap around my arm. *Oh God, I'm caught.* As I slowly turned around, I was surprised to see it was Mrs. Sally. A very furious Mrs. Sally, I must add. "What on earth do you think you are doing child?" she asked me. Mrs. Sally then said, "It is very disrespectful to run off from a party I put together for you."

I just knew she would wonder why I was peaking in rooms in her house. Walking back with me to the party, Mrs. Sally never questioned what I was doing, which struck my attention even more. There is something about that room she didn't want me to see. This party may be keeping me away from that room for now. She is a very mysterious person, and I need to find out what she is hiding from the people of Shelly Grove.

CHAPTER 18

___

As the party went on, I continued to feel uneasy. I didn't like feeling this way. At this point, I was ready to call it a night. But something stopped me in my tracks. I saw the receptionist from Dr Bryant's office standing alone in a corner. She is beautiful as always, wearing a sky-blue mermaid gown that complements her blue eyes.

I immediately rushed over to say hello. I couldn't help but think about the events that had just taken place. I also recalled the receptionist's frightened look when asked about the picture of Mrs. Sally's house that hung on the wall in the lobby of Dr. Bryant's office. Why would she be so afraid to tell me whose house that was? Why would she lie about not knowing why the picture was there in the first place?

I had many questions for her, starting with why she looked so afraid when I asked about the picture. I have bad feelings about Mrs. Sally, and I need to know what secrets she has lingering in Shelly Grove. This house has many secrets, and I can see that now. I need to find the right person to tell me. After our long chat in the lobby, one would think she may open up and tell me something.

I approached the receptionist with a smile because I didn't want to come straight out asking her about Mrs. Sally. I began our conversation with some small talk. "How are you enjoying the party?" I asked.

She looked at me and replied, "It's very nice; Mrs. Sally did an amazing job putting this part together this time."

This time? What does she mean this time? Shouldn't this be the norm because she holds these events for every new person in Shelly Grove?

Smiling at her, she could tell something was bothering me. To break the ice, she finally came out and asked, "So why did you really approach me? I can tell something is bothering you."

I reminded her of the look she gave me when asked about the picture. Taking a deep breath, she chugged the drink she was holding. At this point, I knew something was off.

Scanning the room to ensure no one was watching, she grabbed my hand and said, "Meet me in the bathroom so we can talk."

"Wait. What?"

"Just meet me in the bathroom. Please," she says.

We didn't want to make it seem odd, so she left the room first. Once she was out of sight, I hurried to the bathroom behind her. I was eager to know what she wanted to talk to me about.

As I approached the bathroom door, I wanted to ensure no one was around. I quickly scanned the area to verify no one was watching before I entered the bathroom. Upon entering, I noticed the receptionist leaning over the sink. She appeared as though she was about to vomit. I knew she had just downed her wine, but I wasn't sure why she had that sudden look on her face.

With widened eyes, she tells me, "Something isn't right with Mrs. Sally."

Clearly, but what's not right?

"This woman has many secrets and several people who work for her. You can't trust her Alice," she continues.

"You're scaring me now," I say. "But... I think I believe what you're saying. You see, I just saw something very weird between Mrs. Sally, my boss, Mr. Crammer, and Sam."

"Wait, you saw them together," she asked. At this point, she began pacing back and forth, even more afraid.

I grabbed her, gazed into her eyes, and said, "What is going on? I need to know now."

She couldn't get her words together. She stumbled over every word that tried to come out. Pleading with the receptionist, I said, "Please, I'm begging you, if there's something I need to know, you need to tell me."

She began to cry and said, "You don't know Mrs. Sally like I do. She is nice on the outside but has evil on the inside running through her bones," she explained.

She told me Mrs. Sally is the kind of person you want to keep happy. You must get out of her way if things don't go her way. I understood all that she was telling me but was still very confused.

With my fingers curled under my chin, I began to ponder, "So... if what you are saying is true, why do you think the three of them were standing in the hallway in such a heated conversation?"

Continuing to cry, she says, "It's not safe here Alice. For you, your kids, not even for me. You need to leave this town immediately."

"What do you mean it's not safe?" I ask with my gaze fixed on her.

"I honestly can't say any more. I've now put myself in danger from just talking to you," she explains.

I needed clarification. I had no idea what to think. So many different scenarios were running through my head. But the question remains: *why were the three of them in such a heated conversation?*

The receptionist couldn't tell me anymore. She seemed very afraid, and I could tell she was also fearful for her life. *But could Mrs. Sally be a dangerous person?* I thought to myself. I hugged her and assured her she didn't have to tell me anything else and that I wouldn't tell anyone of our conversation. As she wiped her tears, she thanked me and began to open the door.

Standing in front of us was yours truly, Mrs. Sally. "So we were looking for you Alice, to cut the cake. Why on earth are you two in the bathroom? Together?" she asks. I had no idea what to say. She caught us off guard. At this point, we couldn't hide the fact that we were in the bathroom together.

I looked over at the receptionist. She was lost for words. She tried to devise an excuse for us being away from the party, but I could see how scared she was. She began to stutter, and she couldn't get her words together.

"Well, why are y'all in here?" Mrs. Sally asked again.

I knew I had to come up with something quickly before she realized what was happening. So I said, "She wanted me to show her how I did my eye shadow because she wanted to try it the next time she goes out."

The look on Mrs. Sally's face let me know she

wasn't buying what I was telling her. She was like a dog at that moment and could smell the bull. Instead of asking more questions, she grabbed my hand and told me to come cut the cake for the guests.

As I walked out of the bathroom, I glanced back at the receptionist. She appeared extremely frightened, and I could see the terror in her eyes. I was convinced that Mrs. Sally was hiding something from me. A person doesn't look that scared for no reason.

I have to find my way back here to figure out what secrets lie behind the doors of this house. Mrs. Sally isn't the person I thought she was. *I'll be back, and next time, she won't even know I'm here,* I thought as I looked at her with many unanswered questions running through my mind.

CHAPTER 19

——

The next day, all I could think about was what I had witnessed between Mr. Crammer, Mrs. Sally, and Sam. I couldn't stop thinking about what Mrs. Sally shoved in Sam's mouth. I couldn't stop thinking about that mysterious room at the end of the hall. I couldn't stop thinking about the conversation I had with the receptionist in the bathroom.

Mrs. Sally has a lot of secrets in that room, and I can feel it. I must figure out how to get back into her house to find answers. I knew something was up with her, and my gut told me that this lady was crazy, but my sweet friend Sam had her mother all wrong. Mrs. Sally isn't sweet, and I don't think she cares as much about the people in this town as Sam wants me to believe.

At this point, it was time I got to know my neighbors a little more. So I got up and went next door in an attempt to meet my next-door neighbor. I rang the doorbell and eagerly waited for my neighbor to open the door. To my surprise, Mrs. Sally was the one who came to the door.

With a smirk, she says, "Well, isn't this a nice surprise? Yes, child, how can we help you?" All I wanted to do was scream. She is literally everywhere. I can't get away from her. I couldn't let her see I was on to her, so I had to play the game with her.

I replied, "All I wanted was to introduce myself to my neighbor because I didn't get the chance to meet them at my party." Mrs. Sally then called for the woman currently staying there to come from around the corner.

The clock tower chimed. Once again, on the hour.

Could this really be who I am looking at? The lady I saw standing across the street looking deathly afraid at Mrs. Sally was my next-door neighbor. The look on my neighbor's face was full of fear. I didn't want Mrs. Sally to know I'd seen her before, so I had to play it off. I don't know what Mrs. Sally has done to this lady, but I knew I was not getting any answers from her.

I didn't want it to seem suspicious, so I introduced myself and let her know if she ever needed help with anything. The kids were right next door. My neighbor shook my hand and thanked me for the kind gesture. I turned around to walk away, and looking over my shoulder, I saw Mrs. Sally slowly close the door, looking as if she knew I was up to something. Smiling back at her, I continued walking back to my house.

Something is very strange about this place. My mind took me back to when she took us shopping to find me a dress for the party. It was weird how all the people were standing on the lawns like they were in some trance. I also thought back to the party when everyone stopped like robots and looked up the staircase to watch her walk down the stairs.

Something is wrong with this town; from what the receptionist told me, it must be because of Mrs. Sally. I also think my boss, Mr. Crammer, knows something about her, but how can I get him to tell me anything? My next thought was to visit Sam to see if she could tell me what happened at the party.

I hurried to my car and rushed over to Sam's donut shop. Sam is my friend, and she is a good person. I know she wouldn't sit back and let something terrible happen in this town. She has a good heart and loves all the people in this town. Why on earth would her mom and Mr. Crammer treat her that way?

All these thoughts ran through my head as I drove to Sam's donut shop. When I finally arrived, I saw Sam sitting at one of the tables, gazing out the window. She looked like she was in deep thought. It was time for me to get some answers about Shelly Grove, and I knew Sam would tell me she was my friend after all.

Walking through the door, I greeted Sam and asked if we could talk in private for a moment. The donut shop had several customers, and right now, I really don't know who is working with Mrs. Sally. So, I needed to be careful who I spoke around.

Sam agreed to talk privately, so we went to

the kitchen. With a confused look, she asked, "What's going on Alice?"

I thanked her for being the good person I know she is and for being an amazing friend to me and the kids. I asked her if she could be very honest with me about something. Sam agreed to do her best if she knew what I was talking about.

"The night of the party, I saw Mr. Crammer, who is my boss, by the way, grabbing your arms, and he looked pissed. It looked like the two of you were in a heated conversation. I also saw your mom put something in your mouth, and she also looked pissed. What was that all about?" I ask, getting right to the point.

I just knew she was ready to give me some answers, but instead, she played dumb. The way she looked confused almost had me convinced that she didn't know what I was talking about.

"Um... is it possible that you had too much champagne that night?" she asked. "Could you be overexaggerating?"

I was frustrated with Sam and couldn't understand how she didn't know what I was talking about. I grabbed Sam's arms and pleaded with her to tell me what was happening around here. "Sam, you looked terrified, especially when your mom came to you," I explained.

Sam continued to act as if she had no idea what I was talking about. I thought Sam was my friend, but now I think she may be in on whatever Mrs. Sally and Mr. Crammer are doing in this town. Can I even trust Sam anymore?

Looking at her in disbelief, I said, "Thank you for your time. I'm sorry if I took you away from your work. Maybe you're right; maybe it is all in my head."

Leaving Sam's donut shop with no answers made my stomach feel like it was on a rollercoaster. I sat in my car for a few minutes, trying to process all this. I leaned my head on the headrest of my chair and experienced another flashback—this one more intense.

In this flashback, I saw myself smiling at a girl as we lay in the grass. The experience felt real, but the girl's face was slightly blurry. *Who was that girl in my flashback, and why can't I remember anything about my life?*

As I sat up, I was startled by Mrs. Sally's

gaze fixed on me through my windshield. It was unclear how long she had been standing there, or if she had been watching me since I had made it to Sam's donut shop. I shook my head at her and quickly drove off. Mrs. Sally really does make my skin crawl.

I needed to talk to someone. I have not been in Shelly Grove very long, and this town has gone from being a wonderland to now being something of a Twilight Zone movie. I pulled out my phone and started to call the guy from the party. He seemed like a nice person to talk to.

I hesitated to call him; he stopped, just like everyone else, as Mrs. Sally came down the stairs at the party. Then again, her gown was very mesmerizing. I guess I could understand everyone in the room's sudden pause.

When I spoke to him, he agreed to meet in the park. I'm not sure how long he has lived in Shelly Grove, but maybe he can answer some of my questions. After all, he did say he worked for the police department here, so perhaps he knows more about Mrs. Sally and Mr. Crammer.

CHAPTER 20

—

Approaching the park, I saw him waiting for my arrival. Before stepping out of the car, I stared at him briefly, trying to see if I would get that gut feeling you get about a person, whether they're good or not. I was no longer in tune with myself. I couldn't read him, and that gut feeling never came, but I knew I couldn't continue staring at the guy, so I had to get out of the car.

I hugged him and said, "It's so nice to see you again. At least this time, we're not all dressed up in formal clothing." Trying to create small talk really isn't my thing.

He nodded his head and said, "Uh-huh."

"I'm so happy you agreed to meet me. I'm sorry it was kind of out of nowhere."

"It's no problem at all." He responded. I

could tell he was questioning what this meeting was really about. I mean, we've only met once.

We began to walk through the park. Believe it or not, this town is a lovely place. The grass was always green, and the flowers were always blooming. The clock tower sits right in the middle of the park, which enhances its beauty even more. I couldn't understand how a beautiful place like this could hold so many secrets.

Getting straight to the point, I asked, "So, do you know Mr. Crammer? He was the guy at my party who escorted me and my kids to our table. He also manages the company TelNet."

Eager to hear what he had to say, I peered at him as he searched his thoughts back to the night of the party. Finally, I could tell the light bulb came on in his head as he remembered that night. "Oh yes, I remember him."

"Can you tell me much about him?" I asked. He assured me he didn't know much about him. He said that although this town is small, he doesn't get out much to talk to people. "How about Mrs. Sally? Could you tell me more about her?"

Interesting. Working at the police station, I would have thought he got out a lot, but I guess not.

His gesture at the party and how he kissed Mrs. Sally's hand led me to believe he knew more about her. But his response was a letdown, a disappointment that I couldn't hide.

"Sorry, I don't know much about her either other than that she owns most of the real estate around here. I hate that I can't tell you more about the people here. I know you are probably just trying to get to know everyone here quickly," he says.

"I understand," I say.

"I can only imagine how you feel about moving to a new town and not knowing many people here. But don't worry, I'm sure it will take you no time to become more acquainted with everyone. You seem like a friendly person." He tells me.

Smooth. Real smooth. I smiled at him and nodded in agreement.

Standing there, I remembered what the receptionist told me about Mrs. Sally's many people working for her in the town. At this point,

I wondered if he could be one of them. It does make sense. What better person to have on your side than the police?

The clock tower chimed. Once again, it reminded the people of Shelly Grove that it was the top of the hour. The clock tower is really loud now that I'm standing right here by it. I can see how it echoes throughout the town. I wouldn't be surprised if my ears needed to be checked after today.

That gut feeling finally hit. I can't trust this guy either. He may be working with Mrs. Sally, and I know he won't tell me anything about her. So I quickly changed the subject, and we finished our lap around the park.

Glancing at my watch, I realized time was slipping away. This was the perfect excuse to get away. The kids will be hungry soon, and dinner needed to be prepared. Besides, this guy was of no use to me anymore. It was painfully clear that he was in cahoots with Mrs. Sally. Now, I had to uncover the other potential threats lurking in this town.

CHAPTER 21

—

Lying in bed that night, I wondered how work would be tomorrow with Mr. Crammer. Would he be weird, or would it be weird for me? Should I ask him about the conversation between him and Sam? So many questions are running through my head; I wish I could get one honest response from someone.

As I was lying in bed, I suddenly heard a bang on my window. The bang was so loud it startled me. Adam and Kandice ran into my room, terrified because they also heard the bang. Adam asked me what that noise was and let me know he feared it was a burglar.

Tiptoeing towards my window, I slowly peeked out the blinds to see what that could have been. To my surprise, my neighbor, who I had tried to visit earlier, stood there. She looked terrified. She kept looking behind her as if she knew someone was watching her or was coming to get her. She waved for me to come outside, so I hurriedly grabbed my robe. Rushing for the door, I told Kandice and Adam to stay inside while I went out to see what was wrong with our neighbor.

Slowly stepping outside, I said, "Hello, can I help you? Are you okay?" My neighbor looked frightened. You would have thought she had just seen a ghost.

Fearfully, she asked, "Why did you really come to my house today?"

Even though it was pitch black and the only light we had was from the dim streetlights and the stars in the sky, I scanned the area to be sure no one was watching us. "I have some questions about my landlord. I wanted to see if you maybe knew her very well?"

With a trembling voice, she nodded and told me, "You need to get out of this town. Your family isn't safe here." Her eyes widened, "Leave now, and don't look back if you know what's good for you."

Maybe this lady was a little delusional. Perhaps she had some significant mental health issues. Whatever her situation is, I felt she was being a little weird if you ask me. To be honest, there have been a lot of strange things happening in this town, so I shouldn't be surprised.

"I tried to warn you on several occasions. You probably don't recall this, but I visited you the first night you moved in. I thought you were poisoned because you weren't comprehending what I was saying." She explained.

So it wasn't a dream. There really was a lady standing in my room.

As I looked at my neighbor, it all started making sense. The lady in my dream was wearing a pink sweater, and my neighbor was wearing what looked like the same pink sweater. "So... so you were in my house?"

"That's not important, Alice. Your family is in danger, and you need to get out of here right away!" she says, raising her voice.

I was so confused. I knew Mrs. Sally was crazy, but could it be possible that she was also dangerous? There was no way she could be dangerous, or could she? I started questioning myself.

I was unsure what to say next, so I asked her how I could leave a town where Mrs. Sally seemed to have an uncanny awareness of everything. She couldn't answer me, but she started gazing into outer space out of nowhere. She slowly turned around and walked back to her house. I called for her as she continued walking, but she never turned around to look at me. It was almost as if she was in a trance, her behavior mirroring the others on that strange shopping day.

She was very convincing. This is the second person who told me to leave this town. At this point, I think it's time I listened. So I ran into the house and told the kids to pack only a small bag of the things they needed. They were afraid and had many questions, but I couldn't tell them what I experienced. Screaming at them, I said, "Just do what I said, and don't question me!"

Getting my things together as quickly as possible, I suddenly heard sirens coming through the subdivision. *What in the world could be going on this late at night?* I thought. I peeked out the window and saw several police cars and an ambulance approaching my neighbor's house.

Running towards the front door, I screamed for Kandice to lock the door. I ran outside and saw the EMTs pushing a stretcher towards the ambulance. It looked like there was a body on the stretcher, and they had it covered with a sheet.

I ran over to the officers, questioning the situation. The officers began to reveal to me that they received a call reporting a murder. I could not believe what I was hearing. My heart started beating extremely fast, and tears flowed down my cheeks.

"Please tell me that's not the old lady who lives in this house?" I asked.

"I'm afraid so, ma'am?" The office replied. "Did you know her well?"

I was shocked. *I just spoke to her.*

"No...no, I didn't know her well. My family and I are somewhat new to this neighborhood." I said while trying to wipe the tears flowing from my eyes.

At this point, I had to tell the officers what

had just happened. They needed to know I had just spoken with my neighbor. Before I could get a word out, the one and only Mrs. Sally drove up.

Staring at the scene and looking at all the people standing outside. I knew I couldn't leave Shelly Grove just yet. There were a lot of unanswered questions. I couldn't allow my neighbor's death to go unanswered. Mrs. Sally has something to do with this; I could feel it in my gut.

CHAPTER 22

——

The clock tower chimed. Ugh! It's 7 a.m. Do I really want to hear this chime for the rest of my life? I felt like I didn't get much sleep. Even with the pills Dr. Bryant had prescribed, I still felt like I only got an hour of sleep.

The night before was a horrible experience for me and the kids. They both slept in my bed and expressed how terrified they were. I hugged them very tight and let them know everything would be okay. All I could think about was the fear I saw on my neighbor's face as she stood there on my lawn.

I felt so helpless at that moment. Maybe I should have grabbed her, and we all escaped Shelly Grove. She was the second person in this town who tried to warn me. I hated that I couldn't protect her.

While holding the kids in bed, I saw a car pulling into the driveway through my window. Curious about who that could be, I hurried to the door. When I opened the door, two men with badges stood there. To my surprise, one of the men was the guy I met at my party. Even though I wasn't sure if I could trust him, I was happy to see him. I reminded myself that he works for the police department in Shelly Grove, so maybe he has some news about my neighbor.

"Good morning. What can I do for you all this morning?" I asked as I stood in the doorway in my shorts and tank top.

Reaching out his hand to shake mine, the guy from the party officially introduced himself as Detective Homes. "Hey Alice. This is my partner, Detective Johnson, and we wanted to stop by to ask you a few questions about your neighbor. Do you have a minute?" His voice was low, his eyes darting around as if he was expecting something to happen at any moment.

They began asking me questions like, "Did you see anything unusual last night, or did you hear anything?" Unsure if I could trust them, I told them I didn't see or hear anything out of the ordinary. I assured them this neighborhood seemed safe and had been quiet since we moved in. The detectives handed me their card and asked if I hear anything to please give them a call.

It was tough for me to trust anyone. Could anyone trust anyone at this point? The guy I thought could be someone nice for me seemed just as mesmerized with Mrs. Sally as everyone else in town, the night of the party. I questioned if I could trust the one person in this town I should be able to, but it didn't sit well with me. We tell our kids to always look for a police officer when we see danger, but in this case, can I look to the police?

Standing in the doorway, watching as the detectives drove off, I saw Mrs. Sally drive by and wink at the detectives. She makes me so sick to my stomach. Her smile, so sweet and innocent, hides a manipulative nature. She has everyone wrapped around her finger in Shelly Grove, even the police. Now I know why her house sits at the top of the hill. She controls all that goes on around here. I know now I am not safe talking to anyone here. I must figure out how to get into her house while she is out to find answers.

After that unexpected visit, it was time to prepare for work and the kids for school. We had to go about this day like everyone else. It was just another day, and nothing unusual happened last night.

I reminded the kids that last night was rough, but they must be as normal as possible today. I know that was a lot to ask of them. They were just kids, by the way, and one minute, we were leaving, and the next minute, our neighbor was murdered. It's impossible for them to be normal today. But if only I could tell them I would figure this all out and that they would be okay.

As we approached Adam's school parking lot and entered the drop-off line, I looked back at him and said, "Please don't forget what I told you guys. Nothing happened last night, and you must go about the day like normal."

Adam looked at me with watery eyes, "okay Mom, I will."

I blew him a kiss goodbye and drove off to

take Kandice to her school.

After dropping Kandice off at the middle school, I waved goodbye and rushed to work to see what Mr. Crammer was up to.

Rushing through traffic, all I could think about was my boss. Why did he grab Sam like that at the party? What part does he play in all of this? Could he also be dangerous?

Once I reached my job, I quickly exited my car, dashed through the parking lot, and ran up the stairs to enter the building. Everyone was going about their day like nothing had happened last night. I stood there in the doorway, watching each of my coworkers. Everyone was smiling and having normal everyday conversations.

This isn't right.

No one was talking about what happened. This is a small town. Wouldn't this be top news to everyone? I mean, I would think news like someone being murdered would have shaken up the town, especially since crime doesn't happen here.

Something else caught my eye, though. Detective Homes and Detective Johnson were walking out of Mr. Crammer's office. They handed him the same card they gave me.

Why would they be talking to Mr. Crammer? He doesn't live in my neighborhood.

Once the detectives left, I hurried to my boss's office to find out what they were talking to him about.

"Hey!" I say eagerly. "So... what was that all about?"

"They were here asking questions about you because you live next door to the lady they say was murdered." He stated while twirling a pen through his fingers.

Puzzled, I couldn't understand why they were asking about me. I told them I knew nothing and that I didn't know her well. So why were they snooping around my job and asking questions?

Oh, my goodness. It hit me like a load of bricks. *Is it possible I'm now a suspect? Is it one of those things where you are guilty until proven innocent? Is it possible they know she came to visit me last night?*

So many questions ran through my head at this moment. But I couldn't let that cloud my vision. I was here to get some answers. So, I quickly changed the subject.

Gazing into his eyes, I needed to see if I got the feeling he was lying. "So I was curious; how do you know my friend Sam?"

He immediately stopped twirling the pen and fixed his gaze on me. "Sam?"

He looked a little confused, so I took it upon myself to remind him of their little encounter at the party.

"I Saw you and my friend Sam talking at my party, but I've never seen you two together. She's also never mentioned your name before. I'm just trying to see the connection between everyone here." I say, trying to keep my voice as steady as possible.

Lies were all I was expecting to come out of his mouth, and that's precisely what he delivered: a bunch of lies.

"Oh yes! Sam. Her mom introduced us before the party started and asked if we could help with the décor and food. So that's what you saw us talking about. Sorry, you encountered us in a heated conversation. As you can see, I like fashion and have my own way of doing things. So Sam and I had a little disagreement about how things were going." My boss explains.

It was clear to me he was lying. Who has such an intense conversation over where the hors d'oeuvres and champagne should go? I wasn't shocked that Mr. Crammer wasn't telling the truth; I couldn't get my friend to tell me what was happening with them, so why would he?

"Oh, that makes perfect sense. I see what you mean about liking fashion; you were the whole package that night, Mr. Crammer." I said to him, smiling even though I knew there was more to that conversation between the two of them.

"Well, I probably should get to work. I have quite a bit of reports to get done. Definitely don't want to get on your bad side." I said with a chuckle and walked away.

Sitting at my desk, I started having more flashbacks, but this time, it was a little more horrifying for me. It was a flashback of a lady whipping me with a leather belt. She didn't care where the belt struck me; as long as I was being beaten, it seemed to be all she cared about. I gathered my thoughts and told Mr. Crammer I needed to leave for the day. I told him everything that happened last night was a bit too much for me, and I wasn't feeling well.

In reality, I needed to get out of that office and try to get into Mrs. Sally's house to get answers. Gathering my things quickly, I rushed out of the office. Looking over my shoulder, I noticed Mr. Crammer standing in the doorway, watching me as I walked off. I couldn't let him know I was up to something, so I turned around and waved and assured him I'd be back at work tomorrow. Sipping his coffee, he gave me a nod of approval, and I continued out the door.

Rushing to my car, I knew the only person who may know where Mrs. Sally was at this point was Sam. I almost hit a car speeding out of the parking lot, and I could hear them angrily holding down their horn. I waved my hand out the window, apologizing for speeding, but this person didn't understand how important it was for me to get to Sam's donut shop.

As I rushed through traffic, I kept seeing my neighbor's face. The fear in her eyes. It was clear someone was out to hurt her. I just can't believe she's dead. She tried her hardest to warn me to leave this place.

When I arrived at the donut shop, I was surprised to see Mrs. Sally sitting at a table, reading the daily newspaper and drinking coffee. She looked her usual self, with tightly curled hair and a dress that complemented every curve of her body.

Ugh! I know I wanted to know where she was, but seeing her sitting there made my skin crawl. She is literally everywhere. If I believed in magic at all, I would think she had the power to be everywhere at once.

Entering the donut shop, I looked at Mrs. Sally, waiting for her to make eye contact with me, but she never looked up. She continued to read and pretended she didn't see me standing there. But that's okay with me; the feeling is mutual. I didn't care to see her either.

"Hey Alice! I had no idea you were coming by this early in the day. Is everything alright?" Sam asked as she walked from the back of the donut shop.

"Yes, what makes you think something is wrong?" As if it wasn't weird at all that I was here visiting when I should have been at work.

"Well, usually you're at work during this time." She pointed out.

"Oh right, I got off early today." I quickly replied, hoping she didn't think anything suspicious about my visit.

Brushing off any suspicion, "Well, I'm glad you're here. I wanted to apologize for the other day. I felt bad if I made you feel uncomfortable in any way."

At this point, I knew I had to play along with her. Something clearly is wrong here, and I need to prove it.

"It's fine. Maybe you were right. It's possible I had a little too much to drink that night. We are okay, though. Right?" I ask.

"Great!" Sam said as she hugged me extremely tight as if she was trying to choke me. *Wait, was she trying to choke me?*

"Oh, by the way, I just wanted to say sorry about your loss. I know you are new here, but my mom told me how nice you were to your neighbor.

How you offered to lend a hand if she ever needed help with anything. You are so sweet, Alice." She expressed as she continued to squeeze my neck.

"So, did you speak to her that night? Did you see anyone out there, you know... lurking around?" she questioned.

If only I knew for sure that Sam was being sincere about my neighbor's death. It was evident to me that she wasn't now that she was asking questions about the night my neighbor was murdered.

Gazing into Sam's eyes, I knew what she was really asking. Did I see her lurking around, or did I see her mom lurking around? Whatever the case, maybe the detectives need to ask the two of them questions, not question me. Smiling at Sam, I went along with her little game. I assured her I didn't hear or see anything, just as I told the detectives. Questioning myself at this point, I couldn't help but think Sam was in on the murder as well. I thought she was a good person, but I think she could be just like her mom. *Could Sam be dangerous?*

CHAPTER 23

———

Once again, the clock tower chimed—on time as usual, on the hour every hour. Ugh, at this point, I was ready to climb to the top where the bell sits and bust it myself.

Walking around Shelly Grove no longer felt like a wonderland. My neighbor has been murdered. There hasn't been any arrest, and Mrs. Sally is still walking around here like she owns the place.

It was clear to me that Sam couldn't be trusted, and it was possible she either knew who killed my neighbor or she could be in on it as well. I thought me and Sam were friends. How will the kids feel if they find out Sam is a murderer?

Why would Sam ask me if I had seen anything the night my neighbor was killed? All these thoughts ran through my head, and no official answers remained. I needed to find out her involvement in all of this.

As I sat in my living room pondering, I needed to figure out how to get into Sam's house or her donut shop to find answers. I can't mess this plan up. If she doesn't have anything to do with the murder, then our friendship will be ruined forever.

Since Sam owns the donut shop, she typically closes it at the end of the day. If I could gain access to her donut shop, I might find something useful there. I thought this would be the best way to find some answers, as she spends all her time at that place.

I'm sure I'll find something there if she is involved.

As the day went by, I was eager for closing hours to arrive. I wasn't looking into any random person, but the one person in Shelly Grove that my kids and I fell in love with. I have so many mixed emotions right now. Why did we have to move to a place like this? A place where no one can be trusted. A place where a random old lady can be murdered.

As I sat there in tears, I couldn't bear waiting another moment. I needed to get out of the house. I needed to drive through Shelly Grove and see if I noticed anything suspicious while waiting for closing hours. So, I grabbed my keys and headed out the door.

Walking to my car, I looked over at my neighbor's house. I've never lived next to a house where someone was murdered. You have a different feeling. You feel very sorrowful. It felt as if her spirit still lingered around. She didn't die a peaceful death. I wouldn't blame her if she wanted to hang around to get back at the people who did this to her. I would if I were her.

But I promised myself I wouldn't let her death go until I figured out who killed her. I meant every word, even if that meant ending my friendship with Sam. Even if that meant exposing her mom as the actual murderer she is.

As I drove around town, the people were all the same. They walked the same. They all had smiles on their faces. I thought this place was beautiful, but it is really creepy if you think about it.

Sam says her mom wanted to create a town where everyone got along, a family-like environment, and a community where everyone was close. But as I drove around, I realized she had created a place where everyone feared her.

I drove in circles for hours. I cried many times. I felt horrible. Even though my suspicion about Sam was very strong, I still felt like I was getting ready to betray her.

As I came to a stoplight, I sat there crying. I was crying because I feared what I would find out about Sam. I was crying because I couldn't remember anything about my past or my family. Sam was the only family I had here in Shelly Grove.

"Alice, you can't do this," I said to myself as I continued sitting at the stoplight. *Sam would never do any of these awful things. You know Sam,* I reminded myself.

I knew I Couldn't move forward with this plan. I needed to visit Sam and remind myself why she is the sweetest person here in Shelly Grove. I needed to remind myself of why my kids fell in love with her personality. She is my friend, and friends don't do this to each other. We are supposed to trust each other. If I were her, I would rather work it out than throw the friendship away.

I knew what I needed to do at this point. I needed to visit Sam immediately and have an honest conversation with her. I needed her to know how I felt. I needed her to see how she was being suspicious. Sadly, I also needed her to know how I thought her mom could be capable of murdering another human being.

If our friendship is true, then she'll take what I need to say seriously. She won't get mad at me for blaming her mom for killing my neighbor. She won't get mad at me for thinking she could have something to do with it.

A true friend will listen to me and try to help me realize she has nothing to do with it. A true friend will also hear my concerns about her mom. At least, this is how I think it should go.

As I approached Sam's donut shop, I noticed Mrs. Sally's Rolls-Royce parked outside. I can't stand to see her around here, and I can't stand even to see her car around here. It's gotten to the point where Mrs. Sally is a thorn to me.

I desperately needed to talk to Sam, tell her about her mom, and help her realize who she really is. But I knew I couldn't walk into the donut shop and get Sam alone, knowing her mom was there. So, I decided I needed to wait until she left.

I parked my car farther away to avoid being seen. Waiting in my car for Mrs. Sally to leave Sam's shop was tiring. It felt like I had been sitting there for hours.

NO WAY! NO FREAKING WAY! While patiently waiting, I saw a black sedan pull up to Sam's donut shop. To my surprise, it was the receptionist. "What business could she have here?" I say to myself.

Looking at my watch, I noticed it was closing time. So why would the receptionist be visiting Sam's donut shop this late? The receptionist looked terrified as she told me about Mrs. Sally. She looked even more scared when I mentioned I saw Mrs. Sally, Mr. Crammer, and Sam together. *Why, of all places, would she come here?*

I needed to get a closer look. This may be the secret Sam was keeping from me. It may also be an option for me to find out why the receptionist is really afraid of Mrs. Sally.

Because it was closing hours, the sun had already gone down, so I knew I could use this to my advantage. It was now dark, and I'm sure it wouldn't be easy for them to see from the donut shop's windows. I quickly grabbed my hoodie from the backseat of my car to avoid being seen.

I cautiously crossed the street to get closer to Sam's donut shop, hoping I wouldn't get caught. Walking by, I noticed a pair of sunglasses sitting outside on display from a thrift store near the donut shop. I quickly grabbed them in an attempt to hide my identity.

I slowly put on my shades and covered my head with the hoodie. Then, I peeked through the window to get a closer look. I saw the receptionist, Sam, and Mrs. Sally sitting at a small booth tucked away in a corner.

The receptionist looked scared, Sam looked worried, and Mrs. Sally, of course, had that intimidating look on her face. I desperately wanted to know what they were talking about. I couldn't wrap my head around the fact that the receptionist even agreed to come here and meet with them.

Something wasn't right about this visit. I could feel it. The receptionist may have agreed to come, but I don't feel good about Mrs. Sally's intentions. She's always up to something.

The businesses here were built so you couldn't hear the noise. I could not hear anything they were discussing. I was not good at lip reading, so I had to go off their body language.

I saw the receptionist look at Sam occasionally, looking very surprised. *Was she expecting Sam to help her?* I thought to myself. She would also look at Mrs. Sally with tears in her eyes. I knew something wasn't right about Sam, and this situation proves that to me now.

Then the unthinkable happened. The receptionist got up very angry and pushed the table against Mrs. Sally. She started to storm off when Sam suddenly grabbed her arm. I couldn't hear what was said, but she was definitely upset. She snatched her arm away from Sam and started heading towards the door.

With all the commotion between the

receptionist and Sam, I completely took my eyes off Mrs. Sally. She was no longer sitting at the table. From the angle I was standing, I scanned the room, searching for her. I couldn't see anything.

I desperately needed a better view, so I crawled over behind a bench in front of the donut shop window. From this angle, I could see the entire dining room.

As the receptionist made it to the door, there she was, Mrs. Sally, standing guarding the entrance. The receptionist was startled; I assume she didn't see her move towards the door either.

At this point, I could see the conversation getting even more heated. The receptionist started pushing at Mrs. Sally as if she was trying to get out the door. I couldn't understand why Mrs. Sally wouldn't let her out. I decided the police needed to see this interaction. So I reached for my phone in an attempt to record what was going on, but it dawned on me that I had left it in the car.

"Alice, how could you be so stupid?" I asked myself. This was perfect evidence. The detective could see that Mrs. Sally and Sam were not the friendly people we thought they were. They are holding this girl against her own will.

I felt I needed to do something to help her. But what could I do? How could I get her out of there? "Think Alice," I said to myself. Finally, it hit me: I could act like I was in the area and wanted to stop by to visit Sam during closing hours.

As I was about to emerge from around the bench, the unexpected happened: Mrs. Sally slapped the receptionist. The suddenness of the act left me in a state of shock, unsure of how to react. I instinctively ducked back behind the bench, hoping I wasn't seen. I sat there for a few moments, waiting to assess the situation.

Peeking my head from over the back of the bench, I saw the receptionist wiping her tears from her cheeks. Mrs. Sally grabbed her face in the same way she grabbed Sam the night of my party. I couldn't believe what I saw next. From where I was hiding, it looked as if Mrs. Sally also forced something in the receptionist's mouth, just as she did Sam that night.

I couldn't believe what I had just witnessed

and how stupid I was to leave my phone in the car. This was solid evidence; it was enough for the detectives to look into Mrs. Sally. What she did tonight would have shown them she's not the person she portrays herself as around Shelly Grove.

As I sat there patiently waiting to make sure the receptionist got out alive, a few things were clear to me. It was clear to me that Sam must know her mom is a murderer. It was clear to me that Mrs. Sally was capable of hurting someone. I mean, the way she slapped the receptionist was heartless.

One thing stood out to me the most and hurt more than anything. It was now clear to me that Sam was not the sweet, innocent person I thought she was. She had to be dangerous, just like her mom.

CHAPTER 24

—

After witnessing what happened in Sam's donut shop last night, I felt sorry for the receptionist. No one was in there to help her against that evil lady. The person I thought Sam was, she clearly is not. The Sam I thought I knew; she wouldn't have sat there and watched her mom slap an innocent person.

The receptionist couldn't tell me much about what was happening around here the night of the party, but she clearly knew something. After witnessing the argument between her, Mrs. Sally, and Sam, I see that now. Most importantly, she knows something about Mr. Crammer from her reaction that night. So, I need to look closely into my boss and see what he has to do with all of this.

The best thing for me to do was wait until it got dark outside to avoid being seen. That worked great for me as I spied on them at Sam's donut shop. They had no idea I was there, so I had to wait patiently as the day passed.

Time went by slowly. I sat at work, fixing my gaze on my boss. I was angry. I imagined myself jumping over his desk and slapping him like Mrs. Sally did the receptionist. *Something isn't right about this man.* I thought to myself. He went about his day like nothing had happened in this town. He walked around and joked with his employees. *Oh, please, spare me.*

It was time for me to get off work. I needed to quickly pick up the kids from school and prepare dinner for them. I know my boss, and he's a workaholic. He'd be here all night if he could. I just needed to be patient until the sun went down.

As the evening passed, I informed the kids that I needed to run over to my job because I had forgotten to complete something important.

"Why can't you do it tomorrow, Mom?" Adam asked.

"Well... I need to work on it tonight," I explain.

"Adam, she's a grown woman, don't question her," Kandice chimes in.

"Shut up!" Adam raises his voice.

"Hey, apologize to your sister. Come on, you two, cut it out. Don't you think being a single parent is hard enough," I say.

"Sorry, Mom," they say simultaneously.

"Now I'll be back later, and Adam, Kandice is in charge. Listen to your sister and you two; make sure you all are in bed by 9." I demand.

As it was getting late and close to time for businesses to close around here in Shelly Grove, I hurried back to work to see if I could get any answers about Mr. Crammer. It is possible that he could be one of those people the receptionist was talking about who worked for Mrs. Sally.

He isn't innocent, and quite frankly, he is a little creepy if you ask me. The way he looked at me as I left work was like a lion checking out its prey. I can feel it. You know that gut feeling you get when something isn't right about a person?

Driving back to work, all I could think about

was the heated conversation I had observed between him and Sam. *Were they arguing about who was going to murder my neighbor?* So many thoughts ran through my head, and still no answers.

CHAPTER 25

———

As I approached my job, I decided to park at the end of the parking lot so no one would see my car. If I'm going to get answers, I don't need anyone noticing me lurking around. The detectives are already asking questions about me, so I don't need to give them any other reason to look my way.

This was it! Mr. Crammer was coming out of the building. Approaching him with more questions was no longer an option, so I figured I would follow him this time. I'm sure he has plenty to hide in his house.

Following someone does feel a bit wrong, but there is no place for sympathy in this case. I needed to keep reminding myself of that. Someone has murdered my neighbor, and I need to get down to the bottom of it.

Continuing to follow my boss, I noticed he made several turns and passed many different stores. It felt almost as if we were going in circles. Is it possible he is starting to realize someone is following him? I can't afford for this to go wrong, so I needed to pull back a little. I slowed my car down, allowing another vehicle to get in front of me. Mr. Crammer doesn't seem like a dumb man, and I'm sure he could pick up on it if someone were following him.

Finally, we approached what looked like another subdivision—Whispering Meadows. How ironic, I thought. I wonder if the people in this subdivision have the same suspicions about my boss as I do.

As he approached his house, I decided to park a few houses down. This was my one shot to find out who my boss was. I absolutely couldn't risk being seen, so I brought a ball cap as a disguise.

I slowly exited my car, hoping he wouldn't notice someone following him. As I began to walk, I saw him looking around with suspicion. So, I pretended to be a resident of the house I parked in front of. I walked towards the front door, fiddling my keys to play the part even more. I desperately needed him to think I lived there.

He stood outside, nervously fiddling with his keys for what felt like an eternity. I silently prayed that he didn't notice me tailing him, but his behavior hinted at guilt. Guilty people often feel the need to constantly scan their surroundings.

Finally, this was it; he was going inside his house. I hurried and concealed myself behind a bush in his yard. Slowly, I peered over the bush to gaze through the side window, contemplating how to divert his attention.

As I looked at his car, I noticed a small, blinking red light. This indicated that he must have a car alarm. At that moment, I knew what I needed to do to lure him out of the house so I could sneak in.

Looking around the area, I noticed a small rock. *I've seen this work many times in movies, so maybe it will work for me.* I tested my luck and threw it at his car, hoping it would cause the alarm to go off.

It was just my luck that nothing happened.

"Come on, Alice, what can you do next?" I said to myself. I needed him to come out of the house so I could get in, so I decided to get a little closer this time and pull on the car handle in hopes that this would cause the alarm to go off.

This was it! The alarm went off, and I could hear him rushing through his house towards the front door. I ran back behind the bush so he wouldn't know anyone was there. My heart was pounding, and my hands were sweating. *Was my plan really working? Was he coming outside?*

CHAPTER 26

Stepping out the front door he came out screaming. "Hey! Hey! Who's out here?" My heart began to beat as if it was getting ready to burst out of my chest. He needed to come a little further so I could sneak inside the house behind him.

What the heck am I doing? Sneaking into the boss's house right behind him? Who do I think I am, James Bond? I really hope this works.

Like I said, my boss isn't a dumb man; he knew something wasn't right. I could see he was a little suspicious. This neighborhood seemed like the quiet type—the type of neighborhood where there is little to no crime. I can bet the most that has ever happened here was a squirrel may have been hit by a car or someone lost their dog. He knew this was out of the ordinary. I could see the suspicious look on his face.

"Alice, how could you be so stupid to think this plan would work?" I said under my breath. Shaking my head, I knew I was done for. I knew he was going to see me hiding behind his bushes. I knew I would be going to jail at this point. I'm the outsider in this town, and no one will believe why I'm here.

I sat there patiently waiting for him to decide if he would come closer to check out his car. The car alarm continued to go off, and he stood there staring at it as if he was waiting for something else to happen.

My heart continued to pound, and my hands got even more sweaty. I was officially nervous and scared of what to expect to happen next. Will he be one of those people who will start walking around the yard to see if they can find any evidence why his alarm is going off? Will he be the one who turns the alarm off and goes about his night? Many questions ran through my head, but what concerned me the most was whether I would get caught.

Finally, he slowly walked towards his car, and I knew this was my one chance to get into his house. So, I silently rushed through the front door and tiptoed up the stairs. I knew time was of the essence, so I found the closest abandoned room to hide in.

I stood in the room quietly, waiting to hear him come back into the house. As I stood there, I noticed the same picture that was hanging in my psychiatrist's office on Mr. Crammer's wall. I couldn't help but wonder about the connection. Seeing the picture only deepened my suspicion. I was left with a burning curiosity about the people in this town and their connection to the picture of Mrs. Sally's house.

I started looking around the room to see if there could be any other answers. While searching, I heard my boss walk back into his house. He must have realized it wasn't a burglar because he didn't call the cops. I felt relieved and a little surprised that my plan had actually worked. But now that he was back in his house, I needed to ensure he wouldn't hear me shuffling around in the room.

Continuing my search, I quietly opened the drawers of each nightstand in the room and even checked the closets. He was clean. Nothing was in here indicating that he had anything to do with my neighbor's murder, and there wasn't even anything to show that he was working with Mrs. Sally.

Standing there scratching my head, I couldn't figure out where to look next. My boss was clean. Could it be possible that I had chosen the wrong room? As much as I hate to think about it, but is it possible I was wrong about him?

The unthinkable happened as I stood there pondering how to get out of here without getting caught. The doorbell rang. I looked down at my watch and noticed it was after 9 p.m. *Who could be visiting him at this time?* I peeked out the blinds, and to my surprise, it was Mrs. Sally. I could hear my boss rushing towards the door.

"It took you long enough," he said as he opened the door. He sounded a little frustrated and maybe a little worried if you ask me. As he offered Mrs. Sally to come in, I knew something wasn't right about this visit. I needed to know what the meeting was about, so I slowly cracked the door open to listen in on their conversation.

"You're an idiot!" She yelled. *Why would she be calling him an idiot?*

"How could you let her get close to her at the party?" She asked him.

Who is she talking about?

"Alice is going around asking questions," Mrs. Sally stated.

I knew it. I knew he had some involvement with her. The receptionist was right the whole time. Many people are working for Mrs. Sally in this town, and my boss is one of them.

As I continued to listen in on their conversation, I could hear my boss asking her what they needed to do to shut me up. It is clear to me that these people are dangerous. I now know why the receptionist and my neighbor are scared.

As their meeting continued, I reminded myself of the time; soon the kids would be worried about me. I needed to figure out a way to leave my boss's house. I've heard enough to learn that my boss is working with Mrs. Sally. I slowly closed the door and turned around to lean up against it. I was hurt and scared. I felt alone and didn't have anyone to turn to. In my moment of weakness, I forgot my cell phone was not on silent. Suddenly, my phone rang.

"Shoot! I forgot to turn my cell phone off," I whispered. Shuffling through my pocket, I hurriedly silenced my phone. *I know they had to hear that.* I peeked out the door and could hear them walking towards the stairs.

"Alice, how could you be so reckless?" I asked myself. I needed to think quickly before they came up here. I can't let them find me. So, I quickly exited the room and tiptoed to the bedroom next to me.

As I stood there scanning the room for the best place to hide, I noticed I must have been standing in what seemed to be my boss's room. There was a queen-sized bed with a silky black comforter. Men's clothing was laid across the foot of the bed, and the light was on. *This definitely has to be his room.*

Thinking to myself, I figured hiding under the bed seemed to be the best option in this situation.

So I ran towards it and silently hid, hoping they wouldn't think to look under the bed.

"What are you doing, Mrs. Sally?" My boss asked as they entered the room. She told him she heard a phone ring and felt as if they weren't alone in his house. "You are paranoid," he said to her. "No one is in my house," he expressed.

It was my luck that he had left his cell phone on the nightstand. There must have been an angel looking out for me at this point. It was a coincidence that I hid in the very room where he had left his cell phone.

"See, paranoid," he expressed to Mrs. Sally. As I lay there in silence, I could see his feet as he walked towards what may have been a nightstand next to his bed. He continued telling her the phone she heard ringing had to be his, picking up his cellphone to show her.

I had never felt so lucky in my whole life. I just knew they were going to find me up here. I just knew I was either going to be murdered tonight or I would be going to jail for trespassing.

Finally, they left the room, and I decided to wait there to give them time to head back downstairs. Laying there waiting, I started having flashbacks of a little girl hiding under a bed. She looked petrified, with tears running down her cheeks. She silently held her hand over her mouth as someone entered the room.

I was mentally exhausted from all this sneaking around and from all the flashbacks. I couldn't understand what they all meant. In this flashback of the little girl hiding, I couldn't see anything in the flashback but the person's shoes. *Who was she hiding from?* Snapping back into reality, I was startled by the sound of my boss entering his room again. I needed to devise a plan to get out of here, so I decided to wait until he went to bed before I could sneak out.

While lying there, continuously checking the time, I noticed how many hours had passed and still nothing. My boss hadn't turned off the lights, nor had he stopped moving around. I just knew this was going to be a long night for me.

Man, I have to pee so bad.

Finally, the lights were out, and there was no movement whatsoever. I could hear my boss snoring, which gave me the indication that he was out cold. It was now or never at this point.

Slowly crawling from under the bed, I peeked my head up to confirm he was sleeping. This was my only shot to escape while the coast was clear. He was knocked out, and the door was open. So I crawled from under the bed and tiptoed out the door and down the stairs.

Once I reached the front door, I slowly unlocked the deadbolt and began to open it. My boss lived in what seemed to be an older house, so it shouldn't have surprised me that as I slowly opened the door, it began to make creaking sounds.

I was home free; I couldn't let the door stop me now. So I dashed out of the house and ran to my car. Ducking down in my front seat, I waited a few minutes to see if there was any movement or if he would turn the lights on. *He had to have heard the creaking sound.*

As I observed and noticed no movement, I decided it was time to head home. It was a long night, and I finally knew who else was working with Mrs. Sally. I now know my boss can't be trusted.

I started my car and turned it around. The only way out of my boss's subdivision was to drive back past his house. As I cautiously passed by, my heart skipped a beat at the sight of my boss standing at the window, gazing out. I was unsure if he had noticed me with my ball cap on. The thought that he might have suspected someone's presence in his home sent shivers down my spine.

CHAPTER 27

Yesterday was hard. It was hard to walk around smiling as if the detectives hadn't come to my house to question me. It was hard seeing them in my office talking to Mr. Crammer, especially when he was probably the reason for my neighbor's death. It was hard visiting Sam again and thinking she could be a part of whatever's going on around here.

It was hard walking into the donut shop and watching Mrs. Sally go about her day without shedding a tear for the woman who was just murdered. *Some caring landlord you are, Mrs. Sally.*

I didn't have it in me today to go to work. I really needed someone to talk to. It seemed like the right thing to do was to call my psychiatrist to see if I could visit him today.

I've never been a violent person. I've always tried to see the good in everyone. But this lady is starting a fire in me like never before. Every time I see her, I want to do what I know she did to my neighbor. That lady was sweet and innocent and didn't deserve to die. I have no idea what Mrs. Sally is fully capable of, but one thing I know for sure is she is definitely capable of murder. I have to find a way to prove it.

Shelly Grove is an odd town, and the people here are also strange. Everyone walks around smiling. It isn't normal to be happy this much. Ordinary people have problems and experience anger and sadness, but not here, not in Shelly Grove.

I had to get all this frustration off my chest. I needed to visit my doctor and get some advice. I'm at a point where I want to explode on Mrs. Sally, but if I'm going to figure her out, I have to stay calm. So I jumped out of bed, got myself together, and headed to my doctor's office before starting my day.

As I stepped out the door, I couldn't help but feel the detectives' eyes on me. Their presence near my neighbor's house was unsettling. Ignoring their whispers, I made my way to the car, determined to show them their attention should be on Mrs. Sally's house, not mine.

"Good morning!" I said as I parked my car by the car the detectives were planted in.

Detective Homes nods, "It's a good morning indeed."

"I was in my house trying to piece together the night my neighbor was murdered. Something was brought to my attention from that night." I say.

"Oh really, what was that?" Detective Johnson quickly sits forward with his eyes fixed on mine.

"Well, I just find it kind of strange that Mrs. Sally was in our neighborhood the night of the murder," I explain.

"Why is that strange?" Detective Johnson asks.

"Well, she lives on top of the hill, so what business did she have in our neighborhood that night? Shouldn't she have been home? I mean, she was wearing her robe; shouldn't she have been at home that time of night?" I ask.

The detectives looked at each other and said they would look into it, their questioning expressions revealing their uncertainty. I knew that by planting that little piece of information in their heads, I could divert suspicion away from me long enough to find some answers.

I finally reached my doctor's office and was ready to see a friendly face and talk to someone I could trust. I knew my doctor; I could trust him in this town if no one else. By the way, he does have to abide by HIPPA laws, so technically, he can't go back and tell anyone what we talk about, right?

Eager to see the receptionist, I hurried into the office. To my surprise, she wasn't there, which was weird. She is usually at work, and there are no major holidays that she would need to take off for. *It is the beginning of the week, so why is she out now?*

Standing there, questioning where the receptionist could be, suddenly, my doctor came from around the corner. "Hey Alice, come on back." He waved for me to follow him.

"So, how are you doing today?" my doctor

asked as I began to take my seat.

"I'm doing okay, I guess." I'm not really okay, though. Everything I have experienced since I've been here in Shelly Grove has been a bit overwhelming. I'm honestly ready to kill my landlord myself if the detectives don't hurry up and put her behind bars. I couldn't tell him that, of course.

"I heard about your neighbor. How are you coping with that?" Dr. Bryant asked as he crossed his legs and prepared to write notes when I started talking.

"Well, how does anyone feel after someone is murdered? I mean, I'm doing okay, I guess." I murmured.

"This is a safe place Alice. You can express yourself however you need to. How are you really feeling?" he asked once again as he leaned closer to me to make eye contact.

"To be honest... I'm not alright, and my kids are scared. There are two detectives that think I'm a murder suspect. They keep going around asking all these questions. I've also caught them sitting outside my neighbor's house, but it seems like they're really checking me out."

"I see. I understand how frustrating that is for you. That would frustrate me as well if I were in your shoes. So, did they say why they would think you have anything to do with her murder?" He asked with a curious look on his face.

He is my doctor, after all, so I guess I could trust him. Taking another deep breath, I said, "Well... the night she was killed, she came to my house very scared and wanted to warn me to get out of this town."

Looking at me as if he were trying to read my thoughts, he said, "Wow! That is a lot to take in. I can see how this is messing with your head. Well, I've lived in this town for many years, and I think this is our first murder. Shelly Grove is typically a quiet place—the place you move to, you know, to get away from all the noise, you know what I'm saying."

I nodded, saying, "Yes, I keep hearing that. I... I've also been having those flashbacks again. They are coming more often. It's hard to shake them off."

My doctor sat back in his chair and rubbed

his chin, saying, "So here's what we will do. Because you keep experiencing what seems to be flashbacks, how about I prescribe you medication to help control those? As I did with the first prescription, we will start with a lower strength to see how you respond. If it helps, then we will leave it as is. If it doesn't, then I'll increase it for you. I'll also take you up a notch on your sleeping medication to help you rest more. Seems like you could use some rest right about now."

"Thank you so much. I knew the best thing for me was to come talk to you," I said as I smiled at my doctor.

"Anytime, dear," he replied as he squeezed my hand.

Once our session was over, I asked him where the receptionist was. I told him how much I really liked her and how we always have great conversations when I come in for my visits. But he was unsure where she was. He told me she didn't show up for work today and didn't call out for the day either. *That's odd,* I thought to myself.

After speaking with my psychiatrist, I had that gut feeling that something wasn't right.

After what I saw between the receptionist, Sam, and Mrs. Sally, it was clear something was wrong. Thinking back to the party, the receptionist was terrified. She could barely get her words together to warn me. She was even more scared when Mrs. Sally discovered we were in the bathroom together. I knew something was wrong, but I had no idea where she lived to ensure she was okay.

I asked my doctor where the bathroom was and told him I would be in there a while. I assured him I would let myself out and that he didn't need to walk me out the door. I also figured he needed to prepare for other patients he would see today. He pointed me toward the bathroom and told me to have a good rest of the day.

As I waited in the bathroom for the doctor to return to his office, I had to figure out how to get the receptionist's information. I needed to either call her to ensure she was okay or find her address to check on her at her house. Clearly, going back into my doctor's office wasn't an option, nor was snooping through his belongings.

Exiting the bathroom, I hurried to her desk and began searching for any mail with her name on it. The clock was ticking, and I was acutely aware of the limited time before the doctor returned from his office. I feared getting caught, so I tried to be as discreet as possible, shuffling through any mail or papers on her desk with a sense of urgency.

Finally, I found something! She had a piece of mail lying on her desk with her name and address. 2232 Wade Street. I hurried and started straightening the papers back up on her desk. Suddenly, I heard my doctor coming from his office.

"Oh, Crap!" I said to myself. At this point, I needed to pick up the pace and get her desk looking the way it was when I came in. He would definitely know someone was out here going through her stuff. I didn't need any red flags right about now, so I picked up the pace and pushed all the papers together.

I could hear him getting closer and closer. I was sure I would be caught, so I left the papers where they were and rushed to the bathroom door. At least I would have an alibi, which was me being in the bathroom if he noticed something was off.

As I got ready to enter the bathroom, I heard my doctor's voice come from behind me. It was clear to me that he must know something wasn't right. He had to know I was up to something. But to my surprise, the only thing he said was, "You finally done in there?"

Knowing he thought I had just come out of the bathroom was a sigh of relief. I feared he would think I was the reason for the messed up papers on the receptionist's desk, but I was grateful that some angel was looking out for me again. If he caught me going through her stuff, the police would have a reason to be suspicious of me.

I turn around awkwardly and say, "Sorry. I usually wait until I get home for these things, but I just really had to go." My doctor chuckled at me and told me it was human nature and there was nothing to be embarrassed about. I wished him a good rest of the day and headed for the door.

As I began to open the door, I looked over my shoulder and noticed Dr. Bryant checking out the receptionist's desk. He looked baffled.

He didn't say anything to me, which meant he didn't suspect I had anything to do with the mess, so I continued out the door.

CHAPTER 28

——

Once I left my psychiatrist's office, I could only think about the receptionist. I know she was scared when we last talked, and at this point, Mrs. Sally has to be the one who murdered my neighbor. The receptionist knew more but couldn't tell me. She was fearful for her life and also tried to warn me to leave Shelly Grove. *Oh God, please let her be okay.*

I rushed through traffic, trying to keep up with this stupid GPS. Hearing, "In 100 meters, turn right," irritated me. I wish I knew how to mute the robotic voice and follow the directions on the screen.

My heart was racing as I gripped my steering wheel. Why does it seem like everyone tends to be out when you are in a rush? It seemed like every person in town was on the road today. It felt like it took forever to get to the receptionist's house.

When I arrived at 2232 Wade Street, I didn't know how to proceed. Should I ring the doorbell? How do I explain to her how I got her address? Was I overexaggerating? Could it be possible she didn't feel like coming to work today? I didn't want to scare her and make her think I was a stalker, but I needed to know she was okay. So, with slight hesitation, I approached the door and rang the doorbell.

The suspense was killing me. The receptionist wasn't coming to the door, and the same black sedan she drove the night she went to Sam's donut shop was parked in the driveway, so she must be home. I began banging on the door, but there was still no answer. I was getting worried at this point, and all kinds of bad thoughts were going through my mind.

I peeked inside the window, and it was dead as a doornail. There was no sign of movement. Walking around the house, I noticed the back door cracked open. I was afraid—terrified at this point. *Who leaves their back door open?* I thought to myself.

Stepping into the house, I called out, "Hello! Is anyone here?" The silence that followed was deafening. I called out again, my voice echoing through the empty rooms. "Is anyone home?"

At this point, I began to search the house for the receptionist, proceeding with caution, of course. I recall how terrified she was of these people, and who's to say they're not in the house with me right now?

My goodness, it was almost as if she had never left the house. A plate of food was on the table, and the television was on. I looked at the wall, and a set of car keys was hanging from the key hook.

As I continued through the house, I noticed her purse on the living room table. I thought it could have been an old purse or one she wasn't using, so I rushed over to check it out just to be sure. I honestly thought I was right, but this was her purse. There were many things in there, including her wallet and her license. No one leaves the house without those two essential items.

It was clear to me that something wasn't right here. Was it that she was so scared she left right away, or was she taken? My gut is telling me the receptionist was taken. *But in broad daylight,* I thought to myself? I needed more answers, so I continued searching the house and checking all the rooms.

"Hello, if anyone is here, please call out," I say with a squeaky voice. I was getting nervous at this point. It felt like I was in some horror movie, and some freakishly tall muscular man with a mask on his face would jump out at me any minute now.

Suddenly, the clock tower chimes. I'm startled. It feels like I've literally come out of my own skin. Ironically, the clock tower seems to chime at the right moment. This clock tower is starting to get creepier by the hour.

"NO! NO! NO!" I cried. I finally made it to her room, where I saw her sitting in a chair with her hands tied behind her back. Her feet were tied together, and duct tape wrapped around her head, covering her mouth. Her face was bloody, as if someone had beaten her. She was sitting there lifeless. They had strangled her to death.

I feel like I'm going to be sick.

I shook her body in hopes she would wake up. As I untied her hands and feet, I screamed for help, hoping someone would hear me. I rushed to the kitchen, searching for scissors to cut the tape from around her head covering her mouth. "Wake up, Alice," I told myself; this can't be real. "Was she murdered because of me?" I questioned myself.

I ran back into the room to cut the tape off. She was cold, so she had to be there for a little while. I pleaded with her to wake up. But nothing; she was sitting there lifeless. I cried and cried. I screamed to the top of my lungs, asking myself why. Why would someone kill this girl who was such a nice person? How could someone be so heartless?

"HELP! SOMEBODY, PLEASE HELP!" I continued to scream as I continued to untie her hands and feet.

As I sat on the floor crying and screaming at the top of my lungs, I suddenly heard a loud bang. It was the police rushing into the house.

Someone must have called the police after hearing my screams.

An officer ran over to me, grabbed me, and lifted me off the floor. I was numb, unable to feel anything. Tears streamed down my face as I blinked in disbelief at her lifeless body. My body was in shock, unable to process the reality of what I had just discovered.

As I stood outside, sitting in the back of the ambulance, everything seemed to move in slow motion. I looked at the officers and the crime scene investigators. They were moving in slow motion. I looked at the officers as they questioned people who lived around her, and their lips were moving in slow motion. At this point, I felt like I was in a terrible movie.

Oh God, why is this happening?

Detective Homes and Detective Johnson pulled up to the crime scene and immediately spotted me, both of them quickly making their way over to me. "Oh goodness, what do they want now?" I asked myself.

"So Alice, we were told you were the one who found the receptionist. Is that right?" Detective

Homes asks.

Still numb from the situation, I had no words. I stared into outer space. I couldn't say anything.

"Alice, why do you seem to be around whenever a murder occurs?" Detective Homes asks.

Still frozen, I couldn't say a word.

"Alice?"

Finally, I looked up at him with tears flowing from my eyes and asked, "Does she have any family?" He couldn't give me an answer. I asked him, "Have you checked Mrs. Sally's whereabouts?" Still, no answers.

The detectives stood there looking at me as if I had more information to give them. I just found a dead girl beaten and strangled to death, and these idiots are sitting around letting Mrs. Sally get away with murder. I was furious, and the only thing I could do now was scream. I screamed as loud as I could because, at this point, they weren't answering any of my questions.

Everyone immediately stopped what they were doing from the sound of my scream. The detectives waved at everyone staring at us to assure them they had the situation under control.

"Alice." Detective Homes says softly as he places his hand on my shoulder. "You don't have to scream; you aren't in any trouble here."

I shove his hand off my shoulder. "It really doesn't feel that way," I say sternly as I make eye contact with him.

"We need answers Alice." Detective Johnson says abruptly. "It just doesn't look good that you have been around two people now that have been murdered in this town."

Unapologetically, I say, "You idiots, do you all know anything?" Still no answer. So I stood up and politely said to them, "If you have nothing else to ask me, I'd like to go home and hold my kids now." Detective Homes gives me a nod of approval, and I get in my car and head home.

CHAPTER 29

Later that evening, I took my medication as prescribed and got in bed, pondering the series of events that had taken place so far. Thinking of how the people stood on their lawns as we drove by, it was as if Mrs. Sally had some kind of spell on them. I thought about the kid's first day of school and how weird the staff and their classmates were acting. *Could something like putting a spell on a person be a real thing?*

I thought about Sam's look in the car, almost as if she feared her mom's response. Does Sam know something about her mom that everyone else doesn't know? I thought about what happened between Mr. Crammer, Mrs. Sally, and Sam at the party. I thought about the conversations I had with the receptionist in the bathroom. Then reality finally kicked in: These people really are dangerous.

To top it all off, my neighbor unexpectedly visited and tried to warn me to get out of town. The receptionist also tried to warn me, and now both are dead. I have to form a plan to get into Mrs. Sally's house to figure out what's going on around here.

I picked up the phone and searched my contact list until I found the number I was looking for. This was a long shot, but it was time I started playing their game. I scrolled through my contact list, shuffling through each letter alphabetically until I reached the name I was looking for: Sam's.

Hesitating as my finger hovered over the green call button, I questioned myself for a second. *Do I really want to do this?* I had to remind myself the only way to get answers was to get them away from Mrs. Sally's house. So I did it; I hit the green call button. *It's now or never.*

"Hello," Sam answers.

"Hey Sam!" I say excitedly. "How's it going?" As if that wasn't suspicious.

"Um, good, I guess." She replies.

"Great, so I wanted to ask you a question. Do you...do you got a minute?" I ask.

"Sure. Is everything okay? I saw the news and saw that you were the one who found the receptionist. Murdered? Is that right?" she asks.

"Yep," I say quickly.

"Gosh, Alice, this must be awful for you. Are you alright?" she also asks.

Well, let's see, I moved to a new town. One that I thought was my dream town should I add. Then, oh yeah, my neighbor is murdered in the middle of the night right after she came to warn me to leave my supposed dream town. Let's not forget the other weird things going on around here, like the people mysteriously stopping in their tracks to stare at Mrs. Sally as she drives by or the freakish way everyone stops and stares at her at the party.

Oh, and let's also not forget that the receptionist was also just murdered. Lastly, this is the best part of all, the icing on the cake if you ask me: I'm a suspect in these two murders just because I seem to be around when a murder occurs. Isn't this just nice?

But I can't say any of that to Sam. I have to play it cool. "Yes, I'm fine. This isn't why I called, though."

"Oh, okay. Well, what's up?" She's curious at this point.

"So much has been happening, and I need a do-over. I wanted to extend an invitation to you and your mom. I want to treat you two to a movie. If that's okay with you two, that is." I say.

"If that's okay? What do you mean if that's okay?" Sam questions.

"I mean... I... I'm sorry for asking." I say quickly.

"No. No. Don't be sorry I am saying that sarcastically." Sam chuckles. "We would love to join you for a movie. Honestly, that seems like something we need right about now, especially with all that has happened in this town. We all could use a little laugh. That is if we're going to see a funny movie."

"..."

"Alice. Are you there?"

"Yes, sorry." I really couldn't believe my ears. I couldn't believe my plan was working. "That's great! Let's meet at the theater, let's say, around 11:15 am. Is that alright?" I respond.

"Great! I can't wait. Let me call my mom now and tell her the plan. She's going to be so happy. See you tomorrow." Sam says excitedly before hanging up the phone.

Now, I need to make sure everything goes as planned.

CHAPTER 30

——

I have to make sure this plan goes well. Going over the steps in my head, I needed to assure myself I was doing this for all the right reasons. If these people are dangerous, someone must expose them for who they are. If Mrs. Sally did kill my neighbor and the receptionist, she needs to be rotting in a jail cell somewhere, not walking around Shelly Grove like she owns the place.

The next day, I had to make sure I didn't mess up the plan. As far as I know, Sam has already told her mom about the movies today, and they are both over the top excited about our outing. For things to go smoothly, I needed to enlist help from Kandice.

"Kandice!" I yelled as I stood in the living room, waiting for her to rush down the stairs.

"Yes, Mom. Am I in some sort of trouble?" Kandice asked as she approached the living room.

Apparently, I was standing there with my hands on my waist, as I usually do when I'm getting ready to give the kids a lecture.

Chuckling at Kandice's question, "No honey, you're not in trouble, but I need a huge favor from you today."

"Sure, what's up?" she asked, not realizing that I was about to make my child an accomplice in my scheme.

"So today, I will be taking Mrs. Sally and Sam out to see a movie," I explained.

"Um, okay. What's so special about going to the movies that you will need my help?" she questioned.

"So this is what I need from you; I know you will be in school at this time, but at exactly noon, I need you to text me and say you're not feeling good so I can leave the theater early," I informed her. At this point, I'm pretty sure she probably thinks her mother has officially lost it.

Kandice's jaw dropped. "Wait, so you're telling me you're inviting them to go see a movie with you, just for you to leave them early? I'm really confused Mom. What's the point in going at all?"

I didn't want to confuse her any more than she already was. Kids are like wolves, by the way; they can smell it when something isn't right. So, to put her heart at ease, I told her, "I just wanted Sam and her mom to have some time to themselves. Mrs. Sally always goes out of her way to help others, and she's been under so much stress with our neighbor's death. Sam, well... she always brings you kids free donuts. Why not treat them for a movie?"

Pondering what else to say, Kandice shrugged her shoulders and said, "Sure I guess, if you insist."

I felt bad lying to my child, but this lady had everyone fooled. Even my own two kids like her more than me. I needed to plan this just right for it to work. I hated that I had to drag Kandice into the middle of it, but right now, she is my only hope and the only person I know Mrs. Sally wouldn't question me leaving the theater for.

When Sam and her mom got to the theater, Mrs. Sally hugged me tight and thanked me for treating them to a show. This lady is a murderer, and all I wanted to do was bang my head against hers and repay her for what she did to my neighbor and the receptionist. With a smile, I say, "It's my pleasure. You have been nothing but nice to me and my kids."

Our movie started at 11:30 a.m., allowing us time to enjoy the previews and eat a little popcorn. I couldn't mess this plan up, so I had to sell it and make them think I was enjoying their company. The last preview came on, and at this time, it was 11:50 a.m. I was very nervous and getting a little anxious at this point, waiting for the text from Kandice. *She is only a teenager; will she even remember to text me?* I thought to myself.

The clock tower chimed. Once again, we can always count on the clock tower to keep us on track.

Finally, noon hit, and to my surprise, Kandice remembered to text.

Kandice: Mom, I'm not feeling well. Can

you please come and get me? I think I'm
going to throw up everywhere.

Me: Oh my goodness, sweetie. What did you
eat?

Kandice: I'm not sure. Maybe whatever you
cooked last night.

Me: Okay, I'm on my way.

Kandice: Thanks, Mom. See you soon.

Man, that girl can really sell it. I was thrilled
that she actually texted me. It gave me a little
assurance that this plan might work after all.

Leaning over, I whispered to Sam, "Look." I
showed her the text messages between me and
Kandice. "I need to leave. I'm so sorry, but I need
to check her out of school."

Covering her mouth with her hand, Sam
whispers, "Oh my goodness, Alice, you need to
go. We will be fine. Get her home and in bed."

Sam then told her mom, which was to be
expected. Mrs. Sally looked over at me and
nodded approval, saying that it was okay for me
to leave. I mouthed, "I'm sorry." I quickly grabbed
my purse and headed for the exit.

CHAPTER 31

—

I couldn't believe my eyes—this plan worked! I was so ecstatic! Rushing out of the theater, I headed to my car to go to Mrs. Sally's house.

I'm not going to lie; my hands were a little sweaty. I was nervous this plan was going to fail. I was also nervous driving to Mrs. Sally and Mr. Gerald's house.

As I approached the hill, I got that gut feeling again. Something wasn't sitting right with my stomach. Is my gut trying to warn me to turn around?

But I knew I had come too far to turn around now. Suddenly, it hit me. There is a strong possibility that my car could be seen on the hill heading towards her house. The last thing I needed was more attention on me. How would I explain my reasoning for being on this hill when their house is the only one up here? So, to be safe, I pulled over, parked my car between some trees, and decided to hike the rest of the way up.

This hill is massive. Driving up it is nothing compared to hiking it. It seemed like I walked past the same tree several times. The thought of getting into Mrs. Sally's house was motivation enough to keep me going.

I have no idea what I'm getting ready to get myself into. Is it possible that she's killed more people in this town? I mean, her house is so big; could she have dead bodies stashed in there?

All these thoughts raced through my head, and the one question remained: Where does Sam come into play with all of this? I thought I had a good friend here. But I'm starting to believe the one person that I got so close to, almost like a sister, could be a murderer as well.

Reaching the top of the hill, I couldn't help but feel the strain in my muscles. It was clear I needed to improve my fitness. Perhaps, once this is all over, I'll consider joining a gym.

Now, all I need to do is figure out how to get

in. Standing there with my fingers interlocked behind my neck, trying to configure a plan in my head, I noticed Mr. Geralds's car parked on the side of the house. I reminded myself of how nice of a person he was.

That's when it hit me. I could easily go up to the door and politely ask if I could come inside. Mr. Gerald loves my kids, by the way, so how could he say no to me?

I couldn't understand why I was so nervous. My hands were trembling as I reached out to ring the doorbell. The sound of footsteps echoing through the house sent shivers down my spine. He was coming, and with each step, my heart pounded harder, threatening to burst from my chest.

What if he contacts Mrs. Sally and exposes my presence? The uncertainty was suffocating, and I found myself questioning my decision. Maybe I should turn around and admit defeat. I had no real understanding of the danger I was putting myself in.

As I began to turn around and make my way back down the hill. Suddenly, I heard a familiar voice coming from behind me. I was startled in my tracks. I had already made up my mind that I wasn't going to go through with this. Maybe this was fate. Perhaps I did need to go along with my plan. I've come so far now to give up.

"Hey Alice! It's nice to see you. What brings you up here?" Mr. Gerald said as he stepped onto the porch.

Here I go. There's no turning back now, I reminded myself. "Hey! Yes, it's so nice to see you. I... I couldn't find my wallet, and I believe I left it here the night of the party. I think I remember where I left it. Do you mind if I come in and take a look?"

Mr. Gerald gazed into my eyes as if he were trying to determine if I was lying. I noticed him looking over my shoulders. He was scanning the area when it hit him.

"Where's your car?" he asked.

Shoot. It doesn't look suspicious at all that I came all this way and didn't have my car. I couldn't tell him I hid my car at the bottom of the hill to avoid being seen. I need to come up with something quick.

"My car? Well... I didn't want to get a ticket for driving without a license, so I decided to hike up here."

He wasn't buying that answer. He looked at me, scrunching his eyebrows together. "So you just decided to come all the way up here on foot? You could have told my wife, and she would have gladly brought it to you." He tells me with a grin on his face.

Chuckling, I replied, "I was already out getting some exercise when I remembered I wasn't far from your house. I figured, why not stop by to pick it up?"

This was it. He finally bought my story and let me inside. I told him I wouldn't be long; I just needed to backtrack all the places I was the night of the party. He nodded and said, "Take your time. I'll be in my office working."

Waiting for Mr. Gerald to walk into his office, I pretended to look for the wallet in the dining room where we all sat for dinner. As soon as the coast was clear, I rushed through the house, silently opening each door to see what I could find.

As soon as I heard what seemed to be his office door shut, I crept up the stairs, checking the rooms I couldn't the night of the party. I came across a room that had a bunch of boxes. Grabbing each box, I went through them to see what Mrs. Sally could be hiding in them.

I was utterly puzzled. The boxes contained nothing more than children's clothing and toys. The sight was perplexing—why would Mrs. Sally have such items when her daughter is grown? My confusion deepened as I discovered baby clothes and a blue blanket. This was inexplicable, as Mrs. Sally only has a daughter. The mystery was mounting, and I found myself questioning everything. Sam doesn't have kids, so why would Mrs. Sally have kids' clothes and toys? Why would she have a blue baby blanket?

While searching the rooms, I encountered a room with twin beds. Both beds were covered with white sheets. Trying to remain as quiet as possible, I removed the white sheets. The beds were full of dust. I began to cough, and it was hard to breathe with all the dust flying in the air. *It must have been many years since someone last slept in these,* I thought to myself.

The situation was becoming more suspicious. Why would Mrs. Sally have a blue baby blanket and covered twin beds? It felt as if a dark secret was lurking in this room as if someone had died, and Mrs. Sally was hiding the evidence in plain sight.

Reminding myself that time was not on my side, I knew I couldn't continue sitting in this room. I had many questions, but this was not my priority. So, I placed the sheets back over the beds and closed the boxes. Mrs. Sally surely didn't want anyone to know about this room, so I needed to ensure I left it the way it was.

I tiptoed out of the room and made sure the coast was clear. Standing in the hallway upstairs, I wondered where I should look next. Suddenly, it dawned on me: I remembered the room near the bathroom I was in at the party.

As I hurried down the stairs, I cautiously approached the room. I stood there momentarily, feeling a sense of fear as if something didn't feel quite right. While I stood there, staring at the door, I sensed something unsettling about this room. It felt as if the room was hiding many secrets.

As I entered the room, there was no bed, dark curtains, several chests, and a bookcase full of books. Mrs. Sally isn't fooling anyone; there is a reason for all these chests. I couldn't leave this house without searching all of them, so I went through each chest one by one.

I finally came across one chest that had several pictures. There were pictures of Mrs. Sally standing with four people. What made this photo so interesting was that all their faces, except hers, were scratched out. I couldn't help but take this photo with me, so I folded it and put it in my pocket. "People don't scratch out faces unless they don't want them to be seen," I said to myself.

Continuing to search the chests, I stumbled upon a shoebox full of photos, sparking my curiosity. As I shuffled through the pictures, one in particular struck my interest. A man and woman were embracing a younger Mrs. Sally. Although that picture caught my eye, it was not the one that intrigued me. It was the one of a teenage version of Mrs. Sally. She was seated on a man's lap, his face mysteriously scratched out as well.

I wasn't sure at this point what I had gotten myself into. I was finding things in this house that were very questionable. Shuffling through the photos, I saw a picture of Mrs. Sally and another girl. Mrs. Sally looked extremely happy. I'm talking genuinely happy. I haven't seen her look that way since we met her. But whoever she was with, she also scratched out her face.

The more I discovered, the more I realized Mrs. Sally was harboring secrets. *But how many? And did Mr. Gerald and Sam have any inkling of this?* I couldn't help but wonder.

I continued searching the chest when something suddenly caught my eye. Oh my goodness, am I really seeing this right now? I knew I was suspicious of Mrs. Sally, but to be honest, in the back of my head, I was hoping I wouldn't find anything.

Slowly pulling it out of the chest, I noticed that it was a pink sweater, just like the one my neighbor was wearing the night she visited me.

This was it. This was the evidence I needed. *How could she have her sweater if she was nowhere near her that night?* I thought.

For a moment, I felt terrible, knowing I would be the reason Sam's mom would be going to jail. I would be the reason Mr. Gerald would have to visit his wife behind bars. I had to put my feelings aside and remember I'm here for the greater good, and that's to reveal Mrs. Sally is a murderer.

As I continued searching the room, I looked through another chest. The chest was filled with miscellaneous items, but some things that stuck out to me were ropes and duct tape. I can see people having duct tape in their houses. Why rope?

Thinking back to the receptionist's murder, that is when I realized this rope looked like the same rope that was tied around her arms and feet. I was stunned. Did I really stumble upon all this evidence? I have everything I need right here to put Mrs. Sally away for life. She is a murderer.

I knew Mrs. Sally had something to do with their murders, and I may have found the evidence I needed to prove to the police. Sitting on the floor, I thought there must be more here to show the police that she isn't who she says she is. Suddenly, I felt a breeze from the bookcase, and I noticed it didn't look flush against the wall.

As I stood in front of the bookcase, observing it, I decided to push on it. Surprisingly, the bookcase opened like a secret door. *Why the hell does she have a secret door in her house? Oh my gosh, does she have dead bodies in there? This lady is crazy.*

At this moment, all I could think about was what could be behind this door. I also couldn't stop thinking about poor Mr. Gerald. Does he even know what she's done? Does he know his wife is capable of murder? I had to find out more. So, I opened the door all the way and started to walk in.

Suddenly, I was startled by a sound. It sounded like it was coming from outside the house, and it sounded like it was getting closer by the second. Finally, I was able to make out the sound. It was the sound of sirens. I hurried, closed the door, and rushed to close the chests I had opened.

I knew it was time I got out of this house. I slowly turned the knob on the door and quietly opened it, but it was just my luck; I was struck by surprise. The figure before me was not the devil as they portray in the movies, but Mrs. Sally herself. The shock of this encounter was so intense that my knees trembled, and my hands began to sweat.

She was standing right before my eyes. Her eyes were a lot darker than usual. She looked at me as if she was ready to murder me herself. From the looks of it, I know she knows I've found something. But she was the least of my worries at this point. To my surprise, the detectives walked into the house behind her.

Oh man, what have I done?

"Oh Alice, this does not look good for you, my friend," Detective Homes says as he tugs on his belt.

"Well, isn't this a pleasant surprise?" Mrs. Sally said as she stared into my eyes as if she was ready to rip me from limb to limb.

Stumbling over my words, "Um, hello. I... I was just..." I'm not sure what I should say at this point. I mean, this doesn't look good. They have caught me now at the receptionist's house; I live next door to the old lady who was murdered, and now this. Now, they have found me snooping around Mrs. Sally's house. All I could tell them was what I told Mr. Gerald.

"I was here searching for my wallet, and Mr. Gerald was kind enough to let me in," I tell them.

Mrs. Sally pulls something out of her ginormous purse with a sinister smile. "You mean this wallet?"

My jaw drops, and I'm lost for words. "Where did you find it?"

I should have known I couldn't outsmart a lady who is literally everywhere.

As I stood there, speechless, trying to come up with another story to justify my reason for being here, Detective Homes came from behind Mrs. Sally and asked, "Why do we tend to find you in the wrong place every time we come around? This doesn't look good at all."

"Right, about that." Fiddling with my fingers, I needed to act quickly. He was right; this doesn't look good.

Scanning the room, I could see that this wouldn't end well for me. Each of their eyes pierced into mine. I could imagine Detective Homes and his partner, Detective Johnson, slapping those shiny silver bracelets around my wrist and hauling me off to the police station. I could imagine going through processing as a grumpy officer prepares to take my fingerprints. Worst of all, I could imagine my one phone call to the kids and letting them know what I'd done.

"Alice, are you with us? We found your car hiding between some trees at the bottom of the hill. Why would you hide your car if you were up here just trying to find your wallet?" Detective Homes asked me.

I couldn't tell them Mrs. Sally was evil and had a secret door. So, I thought of the next best thing. "Um, I... I was here trying to get some answers for my neighbor's murder."

Mrs. Sally chuckles. "Murder? Child, are you insane? What on God's green earth would make you think I have anything to do with your neighbor's murder?"

At this point, I had to reveal my conversation

with my neighbor and the receptionist. There was no turning back now, and I had to keep reminding myself that.

"So the night my neighbor was murdered, she came to my house trying to warn me to leave town. She looked terrified. The receptionist also tried warning me at my party. She also looked terrified. The crazy thing is, after both of them tried to warn me, they both ended up dead."

"Uh-huh." Detective Homes says as he scrunches his eyebrows together.

Both of these ladies risked their lives to protect me and my kids. I owe it to both of them to find their killer. There is no time to be afraid of Mrs. Sally now.

"There's one more thing," I say. "Every time these ladies came eye to eye with Mrs. Sally, they had the same reaction."

"And what's that?" Detective Homes asks.

"Fear," I say.

The detectives looked at each other and instructed me to get in their car to talk more about the conversations with my neighbor and the receptionist at the station. As we drove off, I looked back and saw the stare of death Mrs. Sally was giving me. She knows I found something, and I know she will not let this go. *Will I be her next victim?*

CHAPTER 32

—

Speaking with the detectives was rough to do. It was hard to convince them their sweet Mrs. Sally of Shelly Grove was not so sweet after all. The detectives didn't seem very convinced even after telling them about the sweater in Mrs. Sally's house. This shouldn't have been a surprise to me, though. Judging how Detective Homes stared at Mrs. Sally the night of the party tells me a lot. He could either be obsessed with her like the rest of the town, or he could be involved in the murders as well.

She has the whole town wrapped around her finger. *At this point, my doctor seems like the only trustworthy person here.* I thought to myself as I sat in the station, waiting as the detectives whispered to each other in a secluded corner.

"So Alice. I have some information for you." Detective Homes says as he walks back to the table where I was sitting, holding an army green folder. "Hopefully, this puts your mind at ease. We were able to track Mrs. Sally's whereabouts on the night of your neighbor's murder. Turns out she was home during those hours in a meeting for an event she had planned for the town."

But of course, she would have an alibi. I should've never put that past her. She told them she could see the emergency lights from where her house sits on the hill and was concerned. She claimed that was her reason for coming to see what was happening. She also convinced them she had the same sweater as my neighbor. She said it wasn't hard to get the same sweater when there aren't many clothing stores here in Shelly Grove.

Lies! Lies! Lies! That was all that was running through my head. These detectives are on her side. I can't trust anything they say. How do I know they aren't just covering up for her? How do I know they weren't the ones who strangled the receptionist to death?

Sitting in the station listening to all their excuses on why Mrs. Sally couldn't have killed these women, one thought came to mind. *How did they get to the receptionist's house so fast?* Then, it all became clear to me. *I can't trust them.*

I was forming my own opinion about who better to commit a crime than the police themselves. *I mean, they would know more than anyone how to get away with murder, I'm sure.* I thought to myself as I sat there staring them in the face.

"One more thing Alice," Detective Homes says as he looks through that same army green folder. "Mr. Gerald has also confirmed her whereabouts that night."

What! My jaw drops. Are you serious? Who can you trust here? So Mr. Gerald isn't as sweet as I thought. Could he be in on their murders as well? I could understand now why the receptionist told me Mrs. Sally had several people working for her here in Shelly Grove.

How could I be so stupid to think her husband didn't know what was happening around here? As I sat there pondering, that's when it hit me.

Mr. Gerald must have heard me shuffling through their things and called his wife to tell her. How else would she have known I was here?

Mr. Gerald and Mrs. Sally may have the town fooled. Everyone here thinks they are the sweetest people. They believe these two are angels sent from heaven. Now, I can see right through both of them. Mr. Gerald had to help his wife kill my neighbor and the receptionist. I clearly can't trust anyone in this town, so it's time I started gathering my own evidence against them.

I watched as Mrs. Sally and Mr. Gerald left the station. They both looked at me as they walked past me like they were ready to kill me. Looking at the two of them made me sick. They are walking around freely while two ladies are now dead in Shelly Grove. How could the detectives be so stupid? How could they let two murderers go free?

Mrs. Sally always has an alibi, but does Mr. Gerald? As I sat there pondering my next move, that's when it hit me. *I needed to follow Mr. Gerald to see what he's been up to.* You never really see him around town much. They always say he works from home, *but is he really?*

Once I had finished talking to the detectives, I decided to head back towards Mrs. Sally and Mr. Gerald's house. During my drive, I continued having flashbacks. I was startled by the irritating sound of the car behind me banging its horn. I assume I had dazed off at the light during this last flashback. These flashbacks are beginning to feel so real.

This time, I was walking home with friends, smiling and laughing. As I came up to a house that seemed to be mine, a woman whose face was blurry came running towards me and slapped me in the face. All I could do at this moment was cry.

I felt so bad, and these flashbacks felt so real. They have to mean something, and it frightens me that I don't know the meaning behind these flashbacks. Are they a sign? Are they a warning? Continuing to sit in the middle of the road as the cars drove by, tears rolled down my cheeks. I was numb and couldn't move a muscle.

Bang! Bang!

I was startled by someone banging on my driver's side window. "Are you okay?" this lady asked as I continued to sit at the light.

I was falling apart and needed to get my head in the game. I needed to gather myself and get to Mrs. Sally and Mr. Gerald's house to find more evidence. "Thank you, I'm okay," I replied to her. Putting my car back in drive, I quickly headed towards the hill to get to their house.

CHAPTER 33

––––––

As I spotted the bottom of the hill, I realized parking my car a little further away this time would be best. It was one heck of a hike, but I was determined to gather solid evidence. I also needed to start thinking like Mrs. Sally. I understood her well enough to know that she wouldn't make little mistakes, such as parking her car so close and risking the possibility of someone seeing her car. She would do what it took to ensure no one saw her.

Hiking up the hill, all I could think about was what the two of them were up to this time. Who were they planning to murder next in Shelly Grove? Were they plotting to kill me next? How were they planning to kill me, and if I was no longer safe? I need to get this evidence if that means I came every day.

I finally made it to the top of the hill. It was clear to me that walking up to the front door was not an option this time, so I decided to veer off into the woods in hopes I could sit there and observe the area. Finding the biggest tree, I took a squat and hid behind it. It was the perfect spot because I was at an angle where I could see parts of the front of the house and most of the back.

I sat there waiting for what seemed to be hours. I Checked my watch and realized it was getting late, and there was no activity. *Maybe they're trying to lay low for tonight?* I didn't want to get stuck in the woods or even up this hill in the dark. These people are murderers, by the way, and at this point, I don't think anything would stop them from killing me. So, I figured my investigation was coming to an end for now.

As I began to stand up, I started brushing myself off and began to walk, heading back down the hill. Then, all of a sudden, I heard someone coming out of the side door of their house. I hurried and ducked in hopes that no one would see me.

Deep down inside, I desperately wanted to be wrong about Mr. Gerald. I wanted him to be the husband who did as his wife told him. She is the bossy type, by the way. It was very possible she could have killed my neighbor and the receptionist and had him do all the cover-up.

But I saw it right before me with my own two eyes. Standing there in the flesh was Mr. Gerald. He was carrying the same chest I stumbled upon in the room. He dumped the stuff in the chest in the fire pit they had sitting in the back of the house. I couldn't see what he had dumped from where I was hiding, so I knew I needed to get closer.

As I sat there eagerly waiting for his next move, I noticed him fiddling around, checking his pockets as if he had forgotten something. It was just my luck; he must have overlooked the lighter. So he quickly ran back into the house. I knew this was my moment to check the fire pit to see what he was preparing to burn. I had only a few seconds before he returned, so I knew I needed to be quick.

Shaken by the suspense of finding out what

was in the pit, the clock tower sounds one last time for the night so people can get some sleep.

NO! NO! NO! I stood there shaking my head in disbelief, with tears rolling down my face. Is anyone in Shelly Grove a good person? I knew I came to find evidence, but this is all very real now. Mr. Gerald is a murderer, just like his wife.

The rope and the duct tape used on the receptionist were in the fire pit. They were trying to get rid of the evidence because they knew I was on to them. They're trying to cover up what they had done to these innocent ladies. I'm scared now and have no idea what to do with what I just found. The police wouldn't believe me If I told them. I needed solid proof before they burned these items.

As I stood there, I could hear Mr. Gerald walking through the house, which let me know he was getting closer to coming out the door. Remembering my cell phone, I quickly took it out of my pocket and snapped several pictures of what I stumbled upon. These pictures will put the two of them away for life. The police would have no choice but to believe me now.

I hurried to the spot in the woods behind the tree where I was hiding. I sat there as Mr. Gerald walked out of the house. He sprinkled lighter fluid in the firepit. He then lit a piece of paper on fire and threw it in there. I watched as all the evidence went up in flames.

Waiting until he returned to the house, I leaned against the tree and thought about Sam. I wasn't sure what kind of person she was anymore. Deep down in my heart, I still felt like she was a good person. Could it be because I had got so close to her?

Is Sam possibly just doing what her parents are telling her to do? Does she even know her parents are capable of killing someone? Does she know they killed my neighbor and the receptionist?

I had no idea what kind of town I moved my kids to, but it was time we got out of this place. These people will not stop until I'm dead and I can fill it. I needed to get out of Shelly Grove.

CHAPTER 34

——

During my drive home, I drove in silence. I recalled the excitement we all felt the day we arrived here. The kids were super excited, and Shelly Grove felt like the place we could call home. There have been two murders now and no arrests. Mr. Gerald is not the person I thought he was, nor are the detectives. I still couldn't piece together Mr. Crammer and Sam's dealings with all this.

I've seen both of them with Mrs. Sally, which was questionable in both situations. Sam was in the donut shop with her mom and the receptionist, and my boss was in his house with Mrs. Sally. Both conversations seemed intense. But they were definitely on to me.

It was time I got out of this town. As soon as I

pulled into the driveway of our house, I sat there for a second, observing the scene. I looked over at my neighbor's house and wondered what would have happened had I stopped my neighbor from going home, left this town that night, and didn't look back. Would the receptionist still be alive?

I also sat there thinking about the kids. They have started a life here and have real friends who adore them. How will they take the news from me when I tell them we have to move again? Will they hate me? They are just kids, though; they will eventually get over it. Right?

Slowly exiting my car, I press the lock button on the key fob and make my way to the stairs on the porch. Once I approached the door, I fiddled with my keys a bit before finally placing the key in the door's keyhole. I slowly turn the knob, hesitating briefly before I fully push the door open.

Do I really want to do this? Do I really want to break their hearts tonight? Then, I'm quickly reminded of the receptionist's lifeless body. The image of her sitting in that chair tied up, beaten, and strangled to death will forever haunt me.

Yep, we need to get out of here fast.

"Kids, I'm home!" I yell.

"Hey Mom, I'm just up here playing my game," Adam responds.

"Can you two please come here? I have something I need to talk to you guys about!" I also yell as I'm standing at the bottom of the stairs.

I hear two sets of footsteps scrambling through the halls upstairs as I'm standing there eagerly waiting.

"What's up Mom? What do you have to talk to us about?" Kandice questions as she cautiously comes down the stairs. She's probably thinking they're in some trouble at the moment. I usually don't yell for them to come down like that unless they're in trouble.

"For the record, you two are not in trouble," I quickly say.

"Man, Mom, you had me scared for a minute," Adam says as he wipes invisible sweat off his forehead.

"I'm sorry I scared you two. We need to have a serious talk, and it can't wait," I explain.

The kids look at each other curiously.

I reminded them about the two murders that have occurred in this town. I explained to the kids that I was upset because I had become close to the receptionist who was murdered. I also told them this was why I had been coming home late at night recently.

Tears began to form in Kandice's eyes. "Mom, I didn't know you were friends with the younger lady that was murdered. Are you okay?"

"Yeah, Mom, we had no idea. I'm really sorry," Adam adds.

"It's okay you two, but I didn't bring you guys down here to talk about how sad I am; I brought you down here to say..." Oh goodness, how am I going to say this? "I brought you down here to say... I think it's time we leave this town. I don't think it's as safe as I thought."

"So what are you saying? Do we have to move again?" Kandice asks.

I know they won't understand my reason for trying to get them out of this town. They both have settled in their rooms, and I know Kandice loves that little bench in front of the window where she can sit and read an excellent book.

Adam has achieved his goal of becoming the most popular kid in school. *Why is being a parent so hard?*

"I'm sorry guys; I know you two don't want to leave this town, and I know you both have made wonderful friends here, but something isn't right about this town," I explain.

I lower my gaze, pressing my chin to my chest. At that moment, a few tears flowed down my cheeks.

"Mom, it's okay. We trust you more than anyone in the world, and if you say something isn't right..." Kandice looks over at Adam, "then something isn't right."

I immediately raise my head. Hearing those words come out of Kandice's mouth was a sigh of relief.

CHAPTER 35

————

After speaking with the kids, I had them go to their rooms and pack a small bag of essential items. I didn't want to raise any red flags, but we had to travel light.

Those two ladies were adamant about us getting out of this town right away, so that let me know I had to be as discreet as possible. I couldn't let anyone think we were getting ready to escape this town.

"Are you two almost ready?" I ask.

"Coming!" They both yell simultaneously.

Because it was the middle of the night, I felt this was the perfect time to leave. Mrs. Sally can see everything that goes on in this town from her house, so to make it a little harder for her, I turned off all the lights in the house, including the front porch light.

The kids were finally ready, and my heart was pounding. *Was I putting my family in danger by trying to leave this town?* I don't know who Mrs. Sally has working with her, but I know that she is very dangerous.

Finally making it to the car, Adam asked me why we were leaving in the middle of the night and not in the morning. I couldn't tell him our landlord is a psycho killer and is possibly watching us right now. I didn't want to scare the kids either by telling them the two ladies who were murdered also came to me, warning me to leave this town right away.

"It's always easier to travel at night, sweetie," I say.

I extend my finger to press the start button on my car; then the headlights shine instantly. I immediately turn the switch to kill the headlights. "That was close," I say under my breath.

"Did you say something, Mom?" Kandice asks as she tugs on the seatbelt to buckle up.

"Uh, no, sweetie, just thinking out loud," I respond.

As I reserve my car, a little message appears on my dashboard: "Low fuel."

Oh my goodness, just my luck.

I recall this town having a small mom-and-pop gas station open 24 hours. If we are going to get far away from this place, I can't do that on an empty tank of gas. I peek my head out the car window and look towards the hill at Mrs. Sally's house. All the lights are out, so they must be sleeping.

As we exited the driveway and drove in the direction of the gas station, I gripped the steering wheel tightly, feeling my palms getting sweaty. I kept checking my rearview mirrors to ensure no one was following me. I'm not sure if I was being paranoid, but I'm really nervous at the moment. If these women were murdered just for warning me to leave, then what would Mrs. Sally do to someone who actually tries to leave this town?

We finally reached the gas station. It's one of those old-fashioned gas stations with two pumps that only accept cash, not credit cards. The sign is also old-fashioned, where you must manually place the little black letters or numbers yourself.

I pulled up to pump one and turned off the ignition. "Stay in the car," I instruct the kids. "I'm just going inside to pay for the gas."

As I enter the store, the little bell at the top of the door startles me, signaling the clerk.

"Can I help you," a little old lady says as she pops up from behind the checkout counter. She looks like she could be in her 70s. She has salt and pepper-colored hair and is missing two front teeth from the top row. *Why would a lady this old be working at a gas station this late at night? Shouldn't she be in bed somewhere?*

"Yes, I just wanted to pay for some gas. I'm at pump one," I say.

"Uh-huh," she says as she starts to punch in something on her old-fashioned computer. "Why are you getting gas so late at night, child? Don't you know bad stuff happens at night? Especially to a pretty little thing like yourself."

This old lady is now creeping me out. Before I say anything else, I'm reminded of what the receptionist told me: *Mrs. Sally has many people working for her in this town.* "Yes, I... I don't like getting gas when it's hectic in the mornings."

She doesn't look like she's buying anything I just said. She scrunches her eyebrows and says, "So why do you have your kids in the car with you in the middle of the night?"

I look out the store window towards the car and notice how clear it is to see the kids. Adam is sitting in the backseat while wearing his Beats headphones and playing his Nintendo Switch, and Kandice is sitting in the front seat, buried in a book.

I swallow. "We... we are just getting back from a trip, and I didn't want to start my morning off too crazy, so I decided to stop for gas tonight before we got home."

"Uh-huh, well, how much are you trying to pay for your gas?" she asks.

I checked my wallet and found I had two twenty-dollar bills. "I'll put $40 on pump one, please."

As she handed me my receipt, she said, "You really should get home; you never know what kind of murderers are out there. You know there are all kinds of crazy people in the world. People are out here kidnapping women and children, you know. I'd get home as soon as possible if you ask me."

This lady has gone from a little weird to extremely creepy, but to be honest, everything about this town is creepy.

"Thank you so much for the advice. I'll get them home as soon as I get gas." I lie. "You have a good night, and don't work too hard."

CHAPTER 36

Standing at the pump, I watched as the meter counted the gallons of gas and the dollar amount. I was getting nervous as I scanned my surroundings, but as I looked out towards the street, all I could see was darkness. I should be grateful for that, I guess, but there's something about the night when it's pitch black and you can't see anything that gets your imagination going.

Man, this pump is moving very slowly. I really shouldn't be surprised. I should have expected this coming from a gas pump that looked like it came from the 1950s.

Finally, the gas pump clicks and the meter stops at exactly $40. I quickly hang up the pump and shuffle around the car to return to the driver's seat. "Are you two ready?" I ask the kids.

"Yep," Adam replies.

I reach out to push the button to start the ignition. Suddenly, a vehicle comes around the corner and pulls into the gas station. Their high beams are on, and it's blinding. "Goodness, people can be so inconsiderate," I say.

Covering my eyes with my arm, I notice the vehicle pulls right in front of my car. The high beams are still on, and I notice the passenger side door opens. *It's really hard to see. What is this jerk doing?*

I squinted as the high beams blinded me, making my eyes feel weak. I could see the silhouette of a person, but I couldn't discern who was getting out of the vehicle. Suddenly, the high beams turned off and I could see clearly who was standing in front of my car.

It's Mrs. Sally, Standing there in the flesh. Her eyes are piercing into mine. She's wearing these fancy silk navy blue pajamas that look more expensive than any piece of clothing I own.

I tightened my grip on the steering wheel. I considered the option of stepping on the gas and running her over. Perhaps I could reverse as they do in one of those Fast-and-Furious movies and make a quick escape. However, before I could make a move, she was standing next to the driver's side window, waving her hand for me to roll it down.

"Well, isn't this a nice surprise," she says with a sinister smile on her face. "What on earth are you all doing out this late in the middle of the night? Don't the kids have school in the morning Alice?"

I swallow. "Yes, they do. We were just getting gas, so I won't have to worry about it in the morning."

"Hey Mrs. Sally!" Adams says excitedly.

"Oh hey baby." Mrs. Sally scans the inside of the car as if she were the police. "Well, I know the kids could have stayed home in bed, right?"

"Well, Mom thought..." Kandice begins to speak, and then I shoot her a deadly look. "Um, ne...ver... mind."

Who does she think she is? If I wanted my kids at home, they would be at home. Man, I would love to swing my door open hard enough to knock her to the ground. Maybe she should have said that while standing in front of my car; maybe then I really would have hit the gas and run her over.

"Yeah, well, they wanted to ride with me. We also like taking midnight drives through the town, you know, to see what it looks like at night." I explain. "Why are you out so late? Shouldn't you be sleeping? A busy woman like yourself, I'm sure, needs her beauty rest."

She chuckles, "Well, I actually got a call that a light pole hit this small building right before you leave town, and there's sparks flying everywhere."

"What does that have to do with you?" I ask.

"Well child, you see, I own that building, so the police thought I should know what was going on with my property. Gerald and I wanted to come check it out," she explains as she looks back at her husband and waves for him to get out of the car.

Mr. Gerald also walks over to my car with his hands in his pants pockets. "Hey kids," he says as he approaches the driver's side window.

Oh goodness, I could probably take Mrs. Sally, but now her husband is standing here as well. This man is just as dangerous as his wife. Now, all I want to do is get my kids to safety. What if they tried to murder us like they did the receptionist and my neighbor?

Then I remembered we weren't alone. The older lady in the store can see everything going on outside. She'll be a great witness if anything happens; *maybe the police will listen to her.*

I quickly glanced over at the store to see if the old lady was peeking out the window, but I couldn't see her anywhere. Then the unthinkable happened.

"Hey Sally!" The older lady with the salt and pepper-colored hair from the store yells from the door.

"Oh hey, Susan!" Mrs. Sally replies.

Of course, now it all makes sense. That lady must have alerted Mrs. Sally. How else would she know I was here?

Mrs. Sally gazes into my eyes with an evil look. How could I have missed her charade? "Isn't it nice to...." she takes a deep breath, "to know people?"

It's clear to me now. No one can be trusted. Not even the weird old lady at the freaking gas station.

"So... you wanted to come check out the building. Is that safe?" I ask. "I mean shouldn't you wait until the lines are fixed?"

"Well, you're right, but I was trying to be helpful. You see, with the light pole down and sparks flying, no one—I mean no one—can leave this town," she says as she lifts an eyebrow. "So we also wanted to help with getting the roads blocked off."

Wow, it didn't dawn on me the location when she said the light pole fell. There is only one way in and one way out of this town. If the road is blocked off, that means we can't leave, which means I have to stay another day here. I glance at Mrs. Sally as she studies my facial expression. She knows I was trying to get out of here. How in the world did she orchestrate this? How powerful is this woman?

"Unfortunately they said it could take days to fix. They may have to order lines from the next biggest town over." She explains. "The good news is that people in the town can still have power, though! The pole didn't affect those who live in town. Isn't that nice?"

She continued talking, but I could no longer hear a word she said. *How am I going to get us out of this town?* I looked at Mrs. Sally as she rambled on, and that's when it hit me. I don't think she has a few people working for her in this town; I think she has everyone working for her in this town.

— 🫶 —

The kids and I made it back home and sat in the driveway for a few minutes. I stared hopelessly at the steering wheel. What are we going to do?

"Mom, are..." Kandice hesitates, "are you okay?"

With tears forming in my eyes, I look at Kandice and say softly, "Yes." I knew I was defeated tonight, but if I can't get out of here, I need to figure out what's going on in this town.

The kids and I got out of the car and headed back into our house. It was clear to me that I needed to lay low. Mrs. Sally is brilliant, and I need a better plan.

CHAPTER 37

—

I no longer felt safe here in Shelly Grove. Could I be her next target? She must have something planned for me after all this. I couldn't face her any longer, so as days went by, I did my best to avoid anywhere I thought she could be. Even though Sam has the best donuts in town, I couldn't even show my face there, either. I must figure out a way to get more answers.

Mrs. Sally has a secret door in a room behind a bookshelf. There has to be more answers through that door. I decided to lay low for a while and go about my days as usual.

My routines were the same each day: drop the kids off at school, head to work, pick up dinner, and then get ready to start the same routine again the next day. Mrs. Sally has alibis, so it's time I started playing the game her way and ensured I also had one.

Sitting at my desk while at work, I began to ponder the picture I had found in the chest that night. Mrs. Sally had taken a picture with four other people and scratched each of their faces out. Who could she hate that much, or who is she trying to hide that much? Could she have killed those people as well?

"Alice, I need several copies of these papers, and I need them now," Mr. Crammer's voice echoed in my office doorway, his unexpected presence sending a shiver down my spine. "Also, after you're done, these papers must be entered into the system. We are finally transitioning everything to digital."

"No problem," I say quickly.

"Oh, and by the way, your attire is inappropriate for the office. Remember, dress-down days are on Fridays," he says sternly.

I honestly think he knew I was at his house that night; he was staring out the window as I drove by. Could it also be possible that he saw me as I crawled from under his bed? It seemed like he was in a deep sleep—he was snoring, after all.

Lately, he has been coming down on me hard at work. Today, I wore an all-white blouse, some black dress pants, and a pair of black flats. I could see he was trying to find something to get on me about.

The nice, cool, laid-back boss everyone talked about is gone. Now, when he looks at me, it's as if he's ready to kill me right here. I wonder if Mrs. Sally told him about our little encounter.

"Alice, did you hear me?" Mr. Crammer said once more, but this time more agitated.

"Yes, boss, I'll get on it right away. Also, I'm sorry about my attire. I promise I'll try harder tomorrow." I said as I rushed out of my office, gripping the thick paper-filled folder.

As I stood at the copy machine trying to complete Mr. Crammer's impossible task of getting all these papers copied by the end of the workday, it was clear that he was doing this purposefully. I looked down at my watch and noticed we only had two hours left in the workday, and the stack of papers was preposterous.

This was to be expected, though. The moment

they found out I was onto them, I knew I would be the next target. What better way to torture me than at work? Even with all that he has given me to do, I couldn't stop thinking about Mrs. Sally. She has consumed my brain. Each day, I wake up wondering what she is doing or who her next victim in town could be.

My work became my last priority, and I wasn't very active in the kids' interests either. Adam and Kandice are starting to get frustrated with me and think I'm obsessed with Mrs. Sally. I think I need to visit my psychiatrist after I get off work. The office is open until 7 p.m., so I'll have plenty of time.

CHAPTER 38

———

The clock tower chimed. Glancing at my watch, it was now 5 p.m. The end of my workday had finally arrived, and I was more than ready to leave this place. With a detour to my doctor's office on the agenda, I quickly gathered my belongings and made my way towards the exit.

Quickly heading for the door, I bumped into Mr. Crammer. He looked at me and scrunched his eyebrows together. "You need to watch where you're going before you hurt someone, Alice," he says with frustration.

"I'm sorry boss, I was just in a hurry," I tell him.

"Where are you heading in such a hurry," he asked as if he thought I was up to something.

I wanted to tell him not to worry that today wasn't about them. I honestly just needed someone kind to talk to. But instead, I lied. "Oh, I... I um... I needed to hurry to the grocery store. The kids asked me to cook dinner tonight, and I forgot to grab the meat.

Holding his usual coffee mug, he stepped to the side and let me pass. "Please don't let me remind you about your attire again!" Mr. Crammer yelled as I continued out the door.

That guy gets under my skin. I can't wait to be done with these people, but I needed guidance on what to do next. This is why I thought it would be a good idea to see Dr. Bryant today.

My doctor is reasonable. The last time I saw him, he told me his door was always open. If I'm ever struggling, I can just come in as a walk-in.

I learned my lesson from last time. *I will no longer speed out of the parking lot. I almost caused a nasty wreck speeding last time.* I thought to myself as I drove out of the parking lot from my job.

Something surprised me as I was getting close to my doctor's office. I don't wear glasses, but I had to squint my eyes to make sure I was seeing clearly. From the stoplight, I could see the front of the office building, and a familiar car was parked there.

To my surprise, it was Mrs. Sally's Rolls-Royce. Why on earth would she be here? I needed to figure out why she was visiting my doctor's office, so I decided to park around the corner.

I know I said I was trying to lay low, but why would her car be here? I did share a few things with my doctor the last time I saw him. *Oh God, could she be here to get answers out of him and then kill him like she did the others?*

Quickly exiting my car, I began to jog towards the office building. But this time, something stopped me completely in my tracks. Something that I wasn't expecting to see. It was my boss and Sam driving towards my doctor's office. I quickly turned my head so they wouldn't notice me.

My suspicion was even higher now. Picking up the pace, I began to run towards my doctor's office. At this point, I had all kinds of thoughts: Could they all be visiting my doctor to get answers about what information I had shared with him? Is Dr. Bryant their next victim here in

Shelly Grove? I had no idea what to think, but I had to get to my doctor quickly to figure it out.

My doctor's office is in a building with several businesses, and at this point, I don't know who to trust. I needed to be as discreet as possible entering the building, so I grabbed a hat and some sunglasses from this thrift store a few buildings down. I hoped this would help to hide my identity.

Entering the building, my heart was pounding. I wasn't sure what I would find out, but nothing felt good about seeing these three over here. Deciding not to take the elevator, I tiptoed up the stairs so they wouldn't see me coming. The elevator isn't the quietest, especially since these are older buildings.

Finally making it to his floor, I cracked open the stairwell door to see if anyone was around. It was silent, and I could see from where the exit door was that no one was in the waiting room, so I hurried out of the stairwell. The receptionist was dead, so I knew no one would be at the front desk. This allowed me the opportunity to sneak into the office.

Peeping around the corner, I could see my doctor's office door cracked open. The three of them—Sam, Mr. Crammer, and that witch Mrs. Sally—were standing there, all talking to my doctor. I wasn't sure what I should do next. It's just one of me and three of them. I mean, Dr. Bryant isn't that scrawny. I guess we could both take them if we worked together.

I dropped to the ground and crawled closer to hear what they were discussing. It looked like an intense conversation. I could only imagine the questions they were asking Dr. Bryant.

As I leaned in closer, I could hear Mrs. Sally say, "We need to talk about Alice." Oh goodness, please, Dr. Bryant, deny everything. Say I never came to you about anything. Please don't let these people scare you into disclosing what I've shared.

My heart began to race even faster. I'm sure it would burst out of my chest if it went any faster. I needed to do something. I can't just sit back and watch them kill the only person in this town I feel I can trust.

I began to rise to my feet in hopes that if I

just barged right in, they would leave him alone. Suddenly, I couldn't move. I was shocked. It was like someone just took a dagger and stabbed me right in the heart.

"You three are idiots. How did Alice get close to her? She was supposed to be in her house the whole night, drugged and sleeping. One of you dropped the ball, and now we need to cover our tracks," Mrs. Sally says as she continues talking.

But wait. She said you three. There are Sam and Mr. Crammer. From my calculations, that is only two people. She can't be talking about...?

Oh God. Suddenly, I saw Dr. Bryant shove my boss and yell, "You were the idiot who left the back door cracked open at my receptionist's house! I had played it off to Alice like I didn't know where she was for the day. She probably wouldn't have gone inside that house. But thanks to you for leaving the door open; of course, she will go inside."

I quickly placed my hand over my mouth. I wanted to scream. I want to throw up. My stomach felt so weak at this point. My lunch from early literally felt like it was sitting in the middle of my throat, ready to come up.

"You two need to shut up and listen to me. Alice found the picture, and we need to find it before she figures out what's going on." Mrs. Sally says between her teeth.

I wonder what she's talking about. "What does an old folded-up picture with scratched-out faces have to do with any of this? I'm so confused." I say to myself quietly.

She then turns to Dr. Bryant, grabs him by his shirt collar, and asks, "Why aren't the pills working on her? She keeps having those flashbacks. You told me you knew what you were doing. Do I need to hire another doctor because you're too stupid to understand the formula?"

Scanning the room, I look over at Sam and notice she has tears pouring from her eyes. She is pacing back and forth with her hands over her head. Finally, she says out loud, "Please stop! I'm tired of this and don't want to be a part of this anymore."

After Sam said those words, her mom looked over at her and gave her the same stare of death she'd given me before. I could tell she was afraid of her mom. She immediately wiped away her tears and stood at attention as if her mom was a Drill Sergeant in the military.

"If anyone is going to do the name-calling around here, it's me." Mrs. Sally says as she grabs my boss's face and digs her perfectly manicured nails into his cheeks.

"You were supposed to be the right man for the job, and it's your fault that all of this is happening. You let your arrogance get in the way, and the old lady snuck out of the house and made her way over to Alice to warn her. You had one job: to watch her and make sure she didn't leave, and you failed. You all are idiots if you ask me." She also said.

Continuing to listen in on their conversation, Mrs. Sally starts to threaten my doctor and tells him to kidnap Adam and Kandice so she could have some collateral to keep me quiet. I couldn't sit there and listen any longer. I had to call the police to let them hear what they were discussing.

Trying to be as discreet as possible, I pulled out my phone and dialed 911. If the detectives didn't believe me before, they had to at this point.

I needed them to hear their conversation.

I started dialing 911; it felt like the longest two seconds ever before someone came on the line. The 911 representative finally came on the line saying, "911, what's your emergency?"

As I began speaking, I overheard one of them say, "Did you hear that?"

I hurried behind the receptionist's desk to avoid being seen. Could they have overheard the 911 representative come on the phone? I quickly hung up the phone and sat in silence. I could hear one of them creeping around the corner. Now that I know for sure they are all dangerous, I need to figure out a way to get out of this office without being seen.

With my knees to my chest, I sat there quietly with my hands over my mouth hoping no one would hear my heavy breathing. This was unbelievable. I would have never thought I would be in this predicament in a million years. The shock of the situation was overwhelming.

Once I felt the coast was clear, I silently emerged from behind the desk and tiptoed out of the office. I opened the door to the stairwell, and to my surprise, there was Mr. Crammer. He rushed out of the stairwell towards me. Trying my hardest to fight him off, he put a cloth over my mouth that smelled like chemicals.

Things started getting a little blurry. I no longer felt my arms swinging from trying to fight back. My legs then became paralyzed, and suddenly, I could feel my body getting weak. Just as my legs gave in, I could feel my body lifted as if floating in thin air.

Blinking slowly, my vision fading in and out, I could see someone's shoes carefully walking down each step. Then I could hear someone whisper, "Get the door."

I had no feeling in my body. Now I see how it feels for people who are paralyzed. It doesn't feel good at all to not have any feeling in your limbs.

My vision was still fading in and out, but I could see what looked like a bit of daylight. Judging from the amount of light, I could tell the sun was setting. All I thought about was my kids and how worried they would be if I didn't get home soon.

Still blinking slowly, my boss lowers my

paralyzed body down in to the trunk of a car. *Oh God, please help me gain strength. I need help.* In my head, I felt like I was screaming, but no one could hear me.

My vision still faded in and out, and I could finally see all of them standing over me. Mr. Crammer, with his hand, held the trunk up. Blinking slowly, I saw Sam's face. She was frightened and kept asking them why they were doing this.

As I started drifting away, the last thing I heard was Mrs. Sally telling them to get the kids. At this point, I knew I was defeated. All I could think about was what they would do to my kids. *God, please protect them.* I thought before everything went black.

CHAPTER 39

——

Alice! Alice! I could hear someone calling my name as I slowly woke up. Looking at my hands and feet, I noticed I was tied to a chair just as they did the receptionist. Slowly blinking, I saw Sam standing there, attempting to wake me up.

They had my mouth covered with duct tape, so I was unable to say anything to her. I couldn't believe Sam would stoop this low and be a part of this horrible plan. *Are they going to strangle me the same way they did the receptionist?* I thought to myself.

Struggling to persuade Sam to help me, I squealed until she removed the tape from my mouth. "Sam, you have to help me!" I pleaded. She knelt down, her eyes locking with mine, and

302

promised to help me escape, but only if I followed her instructions precisely. I clung to the hope that she still had some goodness in her. Perhaps she wasn't as deranged as her mother, but the uncertainty about her true nature lingered in my mind, casting a shadow of doubt and fear.

Nodding my head slowly, I agreed to do precisely what she said. I had so many questions for her; if I wanted answers and to find my kids, I would listen to everything Sam instructed me to do.

"Where are my kids?" I asked anxiously.

"I'm not sure Alice, but I promise I'm here to help. We won't leave without them, I promise." Sam said sympathetically.

Something in her eyes gave me peace of mind that she was there to help me. I could feel that she genuinely loved my kids and wanted to ensure their safety. I had to be wise, though. Sam wasn't in the clear, and I still couldn't wrap my mind around why she was helping them in the first place.

Every mother has the fear of knowing their children have been taken and having no idea where they are or if they're hurt. My heart was pounding, and all I could think of was if Mrs. Sally had already killed them. Was she saving me for last? Was this her way of torturing me? Sam was my only hope at this point. I had to find some way to trust her to help me find my kids.

"Okay," I say softly.

"Follow me and stay close," she instructs me.

Sam led me down a dark hallway with dull lighting. *Does Mrs. Sally have a hidden basement? Could this be where she hides all her secrets?*

There were rats and spider webs all over the place. I thought I could trust all of these people at one point, but even the man I thought was the sweetest person alive is even a part of this. *Mr. Gerald probably helped them kill my poor babies.*

We finally made it to a well-lit area. Sam told me to wait there as she checked out the area. I stood there, trying to focus my eyes on the dark hallway. I noticed a single dull light bulb dangling from the ceiling. Blinking several times, it looked like it could be another hallway.

"HELP! HELP!" I heard screaming coming from the direction of the dangling light bulb.

Slowly moving towards that direction, the screams got even louder. "HELP! HELP!" It was a familiar voice. So I picked up the pace until I got close enough to realize it was Kandice's screams.

As I approached the area where the screams were coming from, my heart dropped, and I stopped breathing for a second. It felt like someone just came behind me and stabbed me.

Mrs. Sally had my kids covered in chains while dangling in the air over a pool of water. *What on earth did she have planned? Was she going to drown my kids?* Tears ran down my face; I told Adam and Kandice everything would be fine and I would get them out of there.

"Mommy, please help us. You got to get us down from here!" Kandice cried.

Covering my mouth with my hand, I had no idea what Mrs. Sally had plotted. She is a murderer, so killing my kids didn't seem to faze her. I knew I had to figure out how to get them down before Mrs. Sally returned.

Just as I started walking towards the kids, Sam came in and yelled, "Stop! Alice, don't move," she instructed me.

I couldn't understand what Sam wanted me to do. These are my children, and she wanted me to stand there and look at them as they dangled in fear. Has she lost her mind?

"Sam, I have to get them down!" I yelled at her. She assured me we would. She wanted to ensure her mom had no trip wires anywhere that would drop them in the pool.

"The chain she has around them is heavy enough to hold them underwater," Sam told me.

With my heart racing, I continued to scan the room, fearing that Mrs. Sally would come out of nowhere. Trying not to panic, we had to think quickly. Time was not on our side, and we weren't sure when they would return.

As I looked around, worrying if or when Mrs. Sally would walk into the room, Sam and I noticed a lever to lower Adam and Kandice. Sam quickly hurried to the lever and pushed the button to lower them down. I unwrapped the chains from around them and helped them down. At that moment, I didn't care about anything else. I grabbed the two of them and hugged them extremely tight. I just knew they were dead, and

I was next.

"Oh my gosh, I'm so sorry. I was afraid they had already killed you two." I say as I squeeze the two of them in a bear hug.

The kids were shaken up and had no idea who had taken them. I knew time was of the essence, but I couldn't let them go. The scene was too horrific, watching my children dangle in thin air, waiting to be drowned.

With tears running down her face, Kandice says, "Mom, some man came into the house, and I think he drugged us. I was lying on my bed with my AirPods in my ears, reading a book, and Adam was downstairs playing his Nintendo Switch. Next thing I know, this man barged into my room."

"Oh my goodness," I felt sick from hearing what she was saying.

Kandice continued, "As soon as I saw him, I quickly jumped out of bed and tried to shuffle around him. He wrapped his arms around me almost like a bear hug and dragged me downstairs. Once we got downstairs, another man tied a rope around Adams's arms. He was already knocked out. I started screaming at that point for him to wake up, and then all I can remember from there was someone coming from behind me and putting a cloth over my mouth."

Tears were pouring out of my eyes. "I'm so sorry I let this happen to you two. We should have left the night our neighbor tried to warn us. I did this to you guys."

"Mom, this isn't your fault. You don't know these people either." Kandice says as she wraps her arms around me.

"Actually sweetheart, I do know who did this. I've been trying to spare you and Adam's feelings because I know how much you care about her, but Mrs. Sally was the one who took you all. She also had my boss and doctor's help," I explained.

The kids were lost for words, struggling to grasp how the woman who had made all their dreams come true could be the mastermind behind it all. At that moment, the kids and I were brimming with questions for Sam. Suddenly, the sound of a door opening jolted us, and we knew we had seconds to escape before she realized we were gone.

We waited in the darkest part of the hallway to watch and see who would pass by. Adam clung to me in fear, so I held my hand over his mouth, hoping he wouldn't make a sound. Mrs. Sally, Mr. Crammer, and my doctor walked by. Sam was thrilled because she knew there was hope in escaping with all of them down in the basement. As soon as they walked by, we hurried towards the light.

Finally making it to an exit, we came through the secret door behind the bookcase located in the room of Mrs. Sally and Mr. Gerald's house. This was the very room that had all the chests. It all didn't make any sense to me; why would she go through all this trouble just to kill me and my kids? We were new to this town and had no issues with anyone.

Could this be why the house we are renting from her was vacant? Does she have some twisted thought about everyone who moves into this house? Has she murdered every tenant who has lived in that house? Fearful for our lives, so many dreadful thoughts ran through my head. But it was clear that I needed to get us to safety.

Sam didn't want to take the risk of us being seen, so we were able to find a window that could open. I helped the kids out the window first. Then Sam and I climbed out after them. Could this be real? Overtaken with joy, I couldn't believe we made it out. I was thrilled at the thought of getting my kids somewhere safe and finally leaving Shelly Grove.

All I could think about was my poor kids dangling in the air, waiting to be drowned by the one person they loved the most in Shelly Grove. I have no idea what Mrs. Sally's intention was or what she wanted from me, but we were leaving Shelly Grove and never looking back at this place. I know I made a promise to myself to reveal my neighbor's murderer to everyone, but I must do as she wished and *get out of this town.*

CHAPTER 40

———

Running as fast and far as we could through the woods, I knew we had to get somewhere safe. Going back to our house was no longer an option, and going to Sam's donut shop was not safe either. Luckily, we found a small cave to hide in for a while until we could devise a plan to escape Shelly Grove.

I was tired and my feet were killing me. I wasn't sure how long we had been running. It was hot outside, and neither of us had water. This town isn't that big, so I would have thought we would have made it back to town by now. Being lost in the woods is the worst. It feels like you pass the same tree several times.

By this time, it was dark outside, and our only source of light was the moon and the stars.

The kids were scared, and we knew they must have realized by now that we had escaped.

I held my kids tightly as we sat there scrunched up in this tiny cave. I didn't want to tell them this, but I wasn't 100% sure we were in the clear yet. I am their mother, after all, and I needed to remain strong for them. Even though on the inside, I was panicking, I couldn't let them see that. But I was determined, determined to keep them safe and secure.

"Alice, I really need to tell you something. I need you guys to know what's going on around here. I was shocked when I found out, but I had no choice but to go along with them. If I didn't, they were going to kill me the same way they did your neighbor and the receptionist." Sam says as her eyes start to fill with water.

"What are you talking about Sam?" I asked.

"Well... um... everyone here in Shelly Grove has been under a heavy hypnosis. From my understanding, it's been that way for a very long time." She begins to explain.

My laughter at the preposterousness of Sam's claim quickly turned into a plea: "Sam, please, don't waste our time with these wild stories. Tell us the truth. What is the deal with this town, and what does Mrs. Sally have to do with it?"

"Alice, I'm very serious. I know this sounds crazy, but I don't know any other way to explain it. The picture you found with the four people standing with my mom, well, the people in that picture were Dr. Bryant, Mr. Crammer, myself, and..." Sam pauses.

"And who?" I question.

"Well... and... and you," Sam says as she holds my gaze.

"What! This isn't funny, Sam," I say sternly.

"I wish I were joking, I really do," she says softly as she lowers her gaze and begins to fiddle with her fingers.

"Um okay..." I say as I rub my temples.

"My mother's real name isn't Mrs. Sally either. Her name is Lily-Ann, and she is really a resident of a town called Shallow Hale.

Nothing Sam was saying made any sense to me. What makes her think I'm in a picture with all of them when I just met them? Why is she telling me her mother's name really isn't Mrs.

Sally?

Sam's voice quivered as she took a deep breath. Preparing to unveil something that would change my life forever, "I know this is going to sound crazy, but my mom is also your mom. Dr. Bryant's real name is James, and Mr. Crammer's is Cameron. They aren't just random people you met here, Alice; they are your brothers."

It felt like a dagger just went through my chest, and at this point, I was breathing out of control. "What do you mean, Sam? If what you are telling me is true, and these two are my brothers, and Mrs. Sally is my mother, then does that make you my sister?"

She nods slowly, "That's right, I am your sister, and my real name isn't Sam; it's Sarah."

What she told me was surreal, and I felt like I had entered a different reality. I desperately tried to wake myself from this bizarre dream, hoping it was just a figment of my imagination.

Continuing to explain, she told me we were very close, and both dreamed of leaving Shallow Hale. She told me I was the only one brave enough to attempt to leave our mother's presence.

"Wait! Attempt?" I asked, my voice filled with shock and disbelief.

Sam began to reveal more truth. "The night you were supposed to leave, our mother held a going away party, which the whole town was invited to. That is something she has been doing since we were all born. I'm not 100% sure what that's all about, but I think it goes back to our grandparents. I think they were the ones who started this."

"Are you serious?" I ask.

Sam continues, "The night of your party, our mother gave you a glass of what you thought was only wine, but what was really in your glass was something to knock you out."

"Knock me out?" I ask.

"Yes, that's right. She needed you to be sound asleep when you got on the plane so she could hypnotize you into thinking you left. She orchestrated a grand illusion, making you believe our siblings weren't your siblings, and she made you think the airport looked like this extravagant airport. She also made you think the town looked different, and the stores looked different." Sam explains as the gravity of the situation starts sinking in.

"This is beyond belief, Sam," I say, my voice tinged with a hint of doubt.

"You see, our mother inherited all of her parent's fortune. Apparently, our grandparents invented some type of water filtration tablet. Well, the thing about this tablet is that it is the same tablet James has been giving you to keep you under your hypnosis. I also believe that is the same pill they tried to give me, the receptionist, and your neighbor." She goes on to explain.

I couldn't believe what Sam was telling us. I couldn't understand how we were all knocked out when the kids never drank the wine. None of this made any sense to me.

"Alice! Please try to understand what I'm telling you. I know this sounds crazy, and if it were a movie, we'd probably be laughing about this, but unfortunately, this is our reality."

The kid's eyes met mine, their expressions a mixture of uncertainty and belief. It was as if they were slowly accepting the truth in Sam's words.

"Okay, let's say what you are saying is true.

How could she hypnotize an entire town?" I ask.

"Right, so that's what I was trying to say. I think it goes back to our grandparents. I think the people in the town have been hypnotized for many years now. Before, the people in the town were horrible. Strict, if I must add. From my understanding, that's how our grandparents were. This is why I think these people have been this way since they were around." Sam explains.

"You think so?"

"Our mother kept trying to keep you here, and she felt the only way to do that was to hypnotize you and make you believe you were living in a town that was so perfect. Now, all of a sudden, everyone here is so sweet and always smiling," she says.

"This is insane," I mutter.

"The day you boarded the plane, she released a gas to knock out everyone in town, including myself. The clock tower that sits in the middle of the town and chimes at certain hours is a mere reminder, I guess, to keep us hypnotized." She explains.

That makes sense as to why the thing is always

going off.

"From what I'm finding out, once you and everyone else on your flight were knocked out, our mother and brothers came onto the plane and hypnotized you, the kids, and everyone else. They needed them all to think they had flown somewhere completely different." She explains.

"Wait, the day I got on the plane, I think I do recall seeing someone standing in front of me," I say. "Oh my gosh, Sam, I think you're right. I thought it was the flight attendant bringing snacks, but now it makes sense it was our mother."

"I believe this is also the reason for all the parties. I think they are putting those tablets in all the drinks to give somewhat of an extra dose to everyone to keep controlling their minds." She says as she rubs her hands through her hair.

"Oh my goodness," I say as I cover my mouth in disbelief.

"I think this also keeps everyone hypnotized because they are using these water filtration tablets. I mean, think about it: we use water for everything. Our mother's house is the only secluded one, and they have a well. If you noticed, she only drinks water from a glass bottle, and I think it's the same for our brothers," she says.

"How did you come out of your hypnosis?" I ask.

"I'm not sure. All I know is on the day I visited you when you had just moved in, you know, when my mom told me about her new tenants, something changed. The moment I saw you, it was like a pause in the universe and a quick rewind through time for me. All of our past came back to me, and when I noticed you and the kids didn't know who I was, I knew I needed to get answers." She goes on to explain.

"This is crazy. I mean, I couldn't remember anything about my life or my family. All my photos were gone..." I begin to say, and then I'm reminded of one thing. "Wait, all my photos were gone. How did she get rid of all my photos?"

"The day they helped you with your moving boxes, you weren't being very discrete. You had a box labeled 'pictures,' so they took your box and hid it." She explains. "I can bet it's probably in one of those rooms in her house."

As my sister recounts the story of my photos, it all starts coming back to me. "Oh my goodness, I can remember it like it was yesterday. They were there the day we loaded the moving truck with our boxes."

"When you were knocked out on the plane, it was easy for them to take your fingerprint and get into your phone to delete all your pictures. That's why the only pictures you had on your phone were from when you supposedly left," she informs me.

"So why do you think the receptionist and my neighbor were coming out of their hypnosis?" I ask.

"I'm not sure. I'm still trying to figure this out myself. You and the receptionist were really good friends growing up, so maybe when she saw you, the same thing happened to her as it did to me. As for your neighbor, she is very old and used to be all of our kindergarten teachers, so maybe she also had the same experience as I did." She explains.

Sam continued revealing more and more truth to us. She also explained that everyone in town was made to believe they were now in a town called Shelly Grove. She even said our mother made everyone think that we had different names. This was all horrific news.

Was all this true? Is Mrs. Sally really my mom, and are my doctor and boss my brothers? I couldn't understand how my brothers could help her do all of this, but Sam clarified that my brothers were just as cruel as our mother and would do anything to make her happy.

She even said she thinks they used some type of mask to keep from being affected by the sleeping gas. So the three of them were the only ones who weren't hypnotized in this entire town.

She also explained the night of the party, when I saw our mother shove something in her mouth, it was that same pill. I guess they had realized something was off about her and tried to keep her under their control, but to play it off, she made them think she had swallowed the pill and spit it out the moment they weren't looking.

Apparently, she had to go along with the plan to see what our mother and brothers were up to. My poor neighbor and the receptionist were only caught in the middle of all this. They were only trying to warn me, and for that, they were murdered.

The nausea was becoming unbearable, forcing me to lie down and try to process all that Sam had revealed. At that moment, a wave of unease washed over me as I thought about Mr. Gerald. I couldn't help but ask Sam about his role in all of this.

She told us our mother was not really married to Mr. Gerald. Apparently, our father took off when we were very young. Our mother had a crush on Mr. Gerald for the longest time, so to make this town perfect, she had to hypnotize him and make him think he was married to the sweetest woman alive.

This still didn't make any sense to me. I informed Sam of what I witnessed Mr. Gerald doing with the items in the chest.

Sam went on to explain how our mother could make him do anything for her and he wouldn't realize what he was doing. I felt sad to hear Mr. Gerald was also hypnotized, but relieved at the same time to know he didn't know what his wife was capable of. I no longer had to worry that he had something to do with the murders in the town.

At this point, I felt so terrible leaving him there married to a murderer, but I knew I couldn't look back. We had to get out of this place. Once we finally escape, we will try to reveal this town to the authorities so they can come back to rescue Mr. Gerald.

CHAPTER 41

Pondering all that Sam told us, I knew it was time for us to keep walking until we made it out of Shelly Grove. It was dark, and we couldn't see much, so we had to watch our steps carefully. We knew we couldn't get on the roads because our mother's house was on the hill, so we had to hike through the woods to keep from being seen.

The woods are beautiful during the day but creepy at night. We were never sure what we would run into. *Does Shelly Grove have bears?*

Desperate to get out of the woods, we saw a small service dirt road and decided to follow it. As we continued to walk, we saw lights coming towards us, blinding us with their high beams.

We couldn't see anything and didn't know who that was until the lights dimmed. We could finally see it was Detective Homes. I was afraid because I felt he may have also been involved in the murders.

I leaned close to Sam and whispered in her ear, "Do you think we can trust him? I mean, I didn't get a good gut feeling about him. Is it possible he could be helping Mrs.... I mean our mom. Could he be helping our mom out?"

"Oh goodness, no. He was also hypnotized like the rest of the town. She didn't want to risk anything, so it stayed in the family," she explained.

Interesting as it may sound, I was extremely relieved to learn that the detective was another person in Shelly Grove whom our mother had hypnotized. I was thrilled to hear he had nothing to do with her plan. We were unsure if he was still under hypnosis, so we began pleading for his help.

Slowly exiting the car, we could see Detective Homes raise his hand to wave us down. "Hey, what are you guys doing out here in the middle of the woods this time of night?"

Each of us started explaining what was

happening simultaneously, so to him, all he heard was gibberish. To ensure he heard clearly, we allowed Sam to explain what was happening in Shelly Grove and what all our mother had done.

Detective Homes assured us he knew something was up with Mrs. Sally and would get us to safety. I couldn't understand how he felt something wasn't right with her when it seemed they had been on my back the entire time. He informed us he had been going along with Mrs. Sally's game. He wanted to get close enough to her to figure out what she was up to and who she had working with her.

I wonder how his hypnosis wore off.

My curiosity was getting the best of me. I had to ask, "So, how did your hypnosis wear off exactly?" I still wasn't sure if he could be trusted. Something wasn't right about his story.

"To be honest, I don't think I was ever hypnotized. The day things got weird was the day of your party." He starts to explain. "I was doing some inventory in the vault that's located under the police station. When I came out, everyone was knocked out."

"Interesting," I mutter.

"Right! That's what I said. Then, all of a sudden, I hear your mother's voice come over the loudspeaker in town saying all this crazy stuff. She said things like the town's new name and that she only has one child named Sam; it was weird."

I remember Sam telling us she thought the hypnosis went all the way back to our grandparents, *so wouldn't he have already been hypnotized?*

"Look, I'm not sure what's going on in this town. I'm fairly new here myself. Not very many people pay attention to the new cop in town, you know." He says with a chuckle.

Maybe our mother missed him? Perhaps she didn't think to hypnotize him when he first moved to town. Then again, from what Sam told us, our mother had no idea I was planning to leave town until I told her. She probably didn't think to hypnotize anyone else at the moment.

"I think this is all starting to make sense now," I say under my breath.

Continuing down the small dirt road, Detective Homes told us he would get us to safety. He informed us he knew a way out of the town but wanted to stop at the station to let the officers know what was going on with Mrs. Sally and to see if anyone else might have come out of their hypnosis.

While we were heading back down the hill, suddenly, the car came to a complete stop. Standing in the middle of the road was Mr. Crammer, or my brother, should I say. Detective Homes warned us to get down and to be quiet.

Slowly exiting the car, he approached Mr. Crammer and asked him to clear the road so he could pass. Even though Detective Homes says he doesn't think he was hypnotized, I still wasn't sure if the detective was trustworthy. It felt a little suspicious that our brother was standing on the same road we were traveling, blocking us from heading down the hill.

To ensure our safety, I locked the doors as I peeked my head up to see what was going on outside. I couldn't believe my eyes for what I saw next. As the two of them were holding what seemed to be a heated conversation, Mr. Crammer dug a knife deep into Detective Homes' stomach until he dropped to the ground. While he was bleeding out, he tried to warn us to take the car and get out of town.

Suddenly I covered my mouth and froze. I knew we were home free. He would get us to safety, and we wouldn't have to bear another moment in this place. My kids would wake up the next day in a hotel and this could have all been a horrible nightmare.

But no, this was very real. We were faced with a monster, which was my flesh and blood. Sam and the kids screamed for me to get into the driver's seat and run him over with the car. My body wouldn't let me do anything. I had never experienced this type of shock before in my life. I've never killed anyone before. I can barely kill a fly without feeling bad.

This nightmare wasn't over. Coming from the side was my doctor busting the car's windows out with a crowbar. The kids screamed for help as he grabbed them and dragged them off into the dark. I couldn't see anything but Mr.

Crammer standing there with blood dripping from his knife. At this point, Sam and I looked at each other in fear. We knew time was of the essence, and we needed to get the kids back. Sam immediately took it upon herself to jump out of the car and run in the same direction the kids were taken.

I knew what I had to do. I had to kill my brother.

I jumped in the driver's seat, gripping the steering wheel as tight as possible; I hit the gas pedal as hard as I could, running him over. I wasn't sure if that was enough, so I reversed the car and ran him over again.

I've never killed anyone before. Does that make me like my mom? I sat there for a minute, tears running down my face as I processed what had happened. Thinking this entire time, I had a family I couldn't remember, but they were right here under my nose. At this point, I was pissed.

My mother did all this to keep me confined. She did all of this to keep my children from growing up to have a normal childhood. She is a selfish person, and she is a murderer. The love a person is supposed to have for their mother, I couldn't feel that. She made sure of that the moment she hypnotized us all. She is a crazy person, and I finally knew what I had to do to escape her. I must kill my mother.

CHAPTER 42

Slowly exiting the car, I grabbed the knife my brother was holding and headed up the hill to my mother's house. I knew what I had to do to get my kids back. I knew it was time to kill my mom. I knew the only way to free these people from this hypnosis was to get rid of her. Knowing I wouldn't stay in this town, I couldn't bear the thought of what she had planned for my kids. I couldn't bear the thought of what she had planned for my sister, knowing she had helped us escape.

I couldn't let her see me coming, so I left the car parked on the road and hiked the rest of the way up the hill. This was the longest hike of my life. Did she already drown my kids? Did she slit my sister's throat?

All these thoughts raced through my head as I headed towards the house. The front door looked further away every step I took. I knew I couldn't go through the front door, so I had to think of a way to get back into the house. Suddenly, it dawned on me: *the window we jumped out of to escape.*

Tiptoeing up to the house, I had to make sure I wasn't seen, so I sat there for a few seconds to ensure no one came outside. I finally took a deep breath and climbed through the window into the house.

Trying to be discreet, I slowly opened the bookcase door. It was clear to me that if she did anything, it would be done in the basement. The door creaked a little as it opened, but I don't think it was loud enough to alarm them that I was coming.

As I began walking down the stairs into the basement, I was quickly reminded of how dark it was. The hallways were lit with dull light bulbs, and each section had only one single light bulb dangling from the ceiling.

Unsure of their direction, I stood in the dark,

web-filled hallway, silent as a mouse, testing whether I could hear even the slightest sound. I pleaded within myself to please let my kids still be alive. *Could their own grandmother really kill them?*

Finally, I was able to hear someone crying for help. Unsure if that was Adam, Kandice, or Sam, I ran towards the noise until I entered the area I found my kids in earlier. This time, it wasn't just Adam and Kandice chained up; Sam also had chains around her. My doctor, or my other brother, should I add, had a gun pointing toward Sam's head.

"Oh my goodness, please, James... please let them go," I begged my brother.

Coming from out of a dark corner was the devil herself. "Child, now look what you've made me do," my mother announced.

"Please, please," I begged.

"All I wanted for our family was for us to all be together. But you... you little selfish whore had to be the one to try to leave me." My mother said through her teeth.

"Please... please don't hurt them," I cried as

tears poured down my cheeks.

"Oh no. No, no, no... Now you must pay for what you've done, my sweet Alice. There is no time for begging now. Punishment is meant to teach you kids a lesson. You must understand I'm doing this because I love you, dear," my mother said with a sinister smile.

"Please do what you want to me, but let them go. They're innocent in all of this. I was the one who tried to take them from you." I continued to beg.

Looking around, I searched for a way to get to my kids. I noticed my brother standing in a small puddle of water as he pointed the gun toward Sam. I also noticed the messed-up wiring all over the place to light the area. Remembering the knife I retrieved from my brother, I thought to myself cutting the wire could electrocute my brother, and I could free them all.

I knew this plan was risky, and there was a possibility of killing my sister. I thought about running over to my mother and stabbing her in hopes that would change my brother's mind from killing our sister. All these options were very risky, and each of them left the possibility of my kids or my sister being hurt.

As I stood there scanning the room, unsure of my options, I noticed the fear in the kid's eyes. I saw the willingness in James's eyes to pull the trigger and kill our sister. I also noticed the determination in our mother's eyes.

She wants us to be prisoners in this town with her, because of that, she is very determined to do anything to keep us here. At this point, I could hear her loud and clear. She is telling me either we stay here with her, or she will kill me and my kids.

At this point, I felt defeated, and the odds were against me. I knew there was only one thing I could do to save everyone: I had to give in to Lily-Ann, surrender to her, and finally give her what she wanted.

My happiness no longer matters. All that matters is that Adam, Kandice, and my sister are safe. So, I did what any other person would do in this situation: I dropped the knife and fell to my knees. Pleading to let them go, I allowed myself to become vulnerable and give in to my mother's wishes.

Screaming at the top of my lungs, I said to my mother, "I WON'T LEAVE YOU!"

"What did you just say child?" Our mother says with her eyebrows raised.

"I won't leave you. We'll stay here and be the family you want us to be," I say softly, with tears pouring from my eyes.

I assured her we would stay here with her and be the family she wanted us to be. Lily-Ann walked over to me with a smug look and rubbed my cheek with her well-manicured nails. Tugging at her usual dress, which complemented every curve in her body, she knelt on the floor with me, her eyes piercing into my soul.

"I know you didn't think it would be that easy to get away from me," she whispered in my ear.

As tears poured from my eyes, I looked at her and said, "I promise I will not try to leave you ever again. I will stay by your side every day for as long as you live if that means my kids and my sister remain unharmed."

She smiles, "How do I know you're telling me

the truth?"

"I promise, I swear, I will live the life you desperately want me to live. The only way this can happen is if you promise me you won't hurt Sarah or my kids. You must also promise that you won't try to drug us ever again." I demand.

My mother looked at me, then at James, then back at me, and gave that same sinister smile.

Continuing to plead with her, I reassured her we would not try to escape this town again. I promised our mother I would give her what she wanted. We will walk around with smiles on our faces every day and pretend to be the perfect family just for her.

I assured her we would dress to par just for her approval. Promising Lily-Ann that we would speak the way she wanted us to as long as my kids and Sarah could live to see another day.

Tears continued to run down my cheeks; I looked her in the eyes and said, "If I have to give up my freedom and make you happy to keep my children safe, I will do what it takes."

Lily-Ann stood up and put her hand out to help me up. As I rose to my feet, she gave my brother a nod of approval to release our sister and my kids.

Adam and Kandice ran to me and squeezed me as tight as possible. I wasn't sure if I could ever hold them again. My sister looked at me with tears flowing down her face and knew I had to give in to our mother to save them.

If you asked me, it almost felt like making a deal with the devil. From what I've seen, that never turns out well in the movies. But here we are. I've made a deal with the devil herself.

Sarah knew this would continue to be our life for as long as our mother lived. At that moment, the only thing I could do was hug my sister. Squeezing her tightly, I whispered in her ear, "We may be defeated today, but I promise we will find a way out of this town one day."

Sarah looked at me with a bit of relief in her eyes. She knew that as long as I walked the earth, I would go to my grave trying to find a way from under our mother's wing.

CHAPTER 43

———

Minutes bled into hours, hours into days, days into weeks, weeks into months, and months into years. I upheld my pledge to Lily-Ann, not daring to challenge her authority. We lived as she dictated; my children's individuality no longer mattered.

I conformed to her wishes in every aspect of my life. My appearance, my home, my very existence was as she desired. Adam and Kandice were denied their own identities and forced to be Lily-Ann's perfect grandkids. Kandice couldn't express her unique style, and Adam couldn't play the video games he longed for. We lived a life of sacrifice for her.

Lily-Ann wanted to continue to call the town Shelly Grove. She felt Shallow Hale was too depressing of a name and left horrible memories for us. She loves to be in control and wanted to continue living our lives as they were before my sister revealed the truth to us. She feared doing anything different could cause the people in town to come out of their hypnosis.

My brother continued to be the town's Psychiatrist, and my sister had to continue going by Sam and running the best donut shop in town. Our other brother's death was deemed an accident, and the town held a memorial for him as Mr. Crammer. Detective Homes was listed as a missing person, and our mother never revealed his whereabouts to us. Even though our mother's real name is Lily-Ann, she wanted the people to continue to call her Mrs. Sally. She loved having control over the people in this town.

Shelly Grove was her town, and she continued running it how she wanted. The people continued to walk around in a daze. Knowing what was happening to them was too painful to look at anyone. Every so often, I would try to converse with someone randomly in hopes that the hypnosis would wear off just as it did for my neighbor and the receptionist.

To be honest, I think our mother may have increased the dose of the tablets my sister was telling us about. There was no hope for the people in this town. Even when I would have the slightest amount of hope, it was quickly shot down.

The clock tower continued to control the lives of those in this town. It continued to chime every hour on the hour. It was no longer a beautiful sound to my ears, but a painful reminder that I was stuck in this hell on earth.

Mr. Gerald... well, he continued to be the sweetest man. It tore me to pieces every time I saw him. I hated that I couldn't just snap my fingers and get him to leave this devilish woman.

He was the only one in town besides my sister, who made me happy. He always greeted everyone with a smile and was the politest person in that town. He always loved having us over and enjoyed playing with the kids.

I could feel his heart was pure even though he was hypnotized. I could see why our mother wanted someone like that by her side. It's just sad that she had to hypnotize him to get it. He would never be with her if he only knew the evil person he was married to.

Our mother didn't want the town to know we were family, so we continued to act as if we weren't related. We only saw our brother when our mother held an event. My sister and I continued to be close. We were allowed to continue playing that part since the people in the town knew us to be close.

When my sister visited, it gave us a little hope and sunshine. The kids were always so happy to have her over. We never discussed what happened that night because we weren't sure if our mother had any devices planted around my house to listen in on our conversations. We always took each visit as if it were our last, made the best of it, and enjoyed every minute.

Every day was the same: wake up, take the kids to school, go to work, come home, have dinner, and then go to bed. Every day went the way our mother wanted it. We wouldn't dare change our routine without our mother questioning what we were doing. She watched us like a hawk, almost as if she knew I would attempt to leave again one day.

But I kept my promise to her. We stayed and attended every event she held with a smile.

She came over several days each week to have dinner with me and her grandkids. It was always a very uncomfortable feeling in our house when she came. Knowing my kid's grandmother could have it in her heart to murder her own grandkids never sat well with me.

We always had to put a smile on our faces to make her happy, and because her sweet husband, Mr. Gerald, always accompanied her to our house for dinner. We couldn't make him feel anything was going on around here. Our mother threatened she would kill us if he ever found out what she was really up to.

We believed her, too. It was obvious to us that she was capable of murder. Wait, not just any murder, but she was capable of killing her own kids and grandkids.

CHAPTER 44

———

Finally, a day came that was different from any other day in these past few years. Our mother started becoming forgetful. It started small, like forgetting her sunglasses. She never left the house without them. They were her signature accessory, making her feel and look like a woman of mystery.

Then she started missing nail and hair appointments. With her falling off her routine, the townspeople now walked around confused. Some people didn't know what house theirs was or what car was theirs. Things became very weird in the town. People stopped walking around with that very painful smile on their faces and started looking like real human beings. No one walks around all day, every day, smiling.

I started to question what was going on in the town, so I reached out to my sister to get together to figure it out. We met at my house, trying to piece together what was going on.

Sitting in the living room, chatting about what had been happening in town, my phone suddenly rang. I reached into the back pocket of my blue jeans to grab my phone and instantly felt that something was off. I rarely receive calls unless they're from my sister. Our mother often shows up uninvited, so I knew it couldn't have been her.

"Hello," I say.

A familiar voice was on the other end, filled with urgency: "Alice! Alice! I really need you and Sam to... to come..."

"To come where? And who is this?" I ask. The voice sounded somewhat muffled on the other end.

"This is James." He whispered.

Instantly rising to my feet. I covered the speaker with my hand and mouthed to my sister that James was on the phone.

"James? What do you need?" I asked.

"It's about mom. She's not doing so well. I need you guys to come down to the hospital. She's been admitted." He says.

"Admitted? To the hospital?" I ask.

"Just get here quick. It doesn't look good. Something is seriously wrong with her." He said while sniffling as if he were crying.

Are people like James and our mother even capable of producing tears? I questioned myself.

"Um... okay, James. We are on our way." I say just before pushing the red button on my screen to end the call.

"What's going on?" My sister asked as I placed my phone back in my back pocket.

"That was James, and he said we needed to get to the hospital immediately because mom has been admitted. He says it looks bad," I explain.

We stared at each other for a brief second. We were shocked by the phone call I had just received and unsure how to proceed.

Looking at my sister, I could see a corner of her mouth rise just a bit as if she wanted to give off a tiny smile.

"Not yet. We're not sure what's going on.

We can't get too happy just yet," I say, injecting a note of caution that causes her almost smile to disappear, replaced by a flicker of uncertainty.

Continuing to stand there in shock, I had many questions. Could this really be happening right now? Are we getting ready to be free of our mother? Is it possible she could be dying?

"Alice, are our dreams getting ready to come true?" My sister asked.

"I'm not sure, but the only way for us to find out is to go to the hospital," I say.

She nodded at me in agreement. She knew I was right and that seeing her under our own will was the only way we would find out if what James was saying was true.

"Kids, we will be right back!" I yelled, and we hurried out the door.

Driving to the hospital, we had the weirdest experience. Everyone in the town was headed in the same direction. As we pulled into the parking lot of the hospital, everyone in the town stood in front of the emergency room entrance, staring at the doors.

We tried talking to people, but it was as if

no one could hear us. The town just shut down completely, and everyone was there.

The clock tower chimes once again.

Looking down at my watch, I noticed it was 5 p.m. We looked at each other with fear in our eyes. Then we looked in the direction of the clock tower. Something felt different. For some reason, the chime felt less intimidating.

As we approached the entrance, my sister and I held hands unsure of what to expect once we enter our mother's room. My sister looked at me and asked, "Could this be our opportunity to leave this town?"

I wasn't sure of what to say, so I reassured her that I will always keep trying to find a way out of this town no matter what happens.

Squeezing each other's hands, we stepped through the hospital doors. The staff stared at us as if we were preparing to walk on death row.

"Hello. We were told Mrs. Sally was admitted here. Can you tell us what room she is in, please?" I asked one of the ladies sitting at the front desk.

With a somewhat blank look, she says, "Room 222A."

Slowly walking the halls, my sister and I kept our eyes straight and did not make eye contact with anyone in the hospital. It honestly felt like we were moving in slow motion, and the people around us were frozen in time.

We approached the elevator, and I slowly extended my finger out to press the silver button with the bold number two. We silently stood there as the elevator lifted us to the second floor.

Ding!

The elevator door slowly opened. The hallway was dark and quiet. No one was in sight, and it almost looked like this floor was vacant.

Looking at my sister, I placed my hand into hers, interlocking our fingers. I reminded her, "Remember, whatever happens, I'll never give up trying."

She looked at me and gave off a smile. "I know you won't."

We slowly walked down the hall and came to what seemed to be a split in the hallway. On the wall in front of us was a placard with a single arrow pointing to the right for rooms 200-211 and another arrow pointing to the left for rooms

212-222.

I nodded my head towards the hallway to the left. "This way," I say.

Looking at every door as we walked by, we counted the numbers on the placards one by one. 212A, 213A, 214A... until finally we made it to 222A.

We looked at each other one last time, and I swallowed what felt like a lump in my throat. Reminding my sister one last time, I said, "Remember, whatever happens, I'll never give up trying."

She nodded in agreement, and we slowly opened the door.

Entering our mother's room, we found our brother was pacing back and forth, worried. Mr. Gerald was sitting in a chair, holding our mother's hand. Our mother was lying in bed, staring into outer space.

We walked over to our mother's bed and realized how bad of a condition she was in. She didn't even respond to our presence. She would have usually said something slick like, "Why are you looking at me like I'm an idiot child? Do you think I'm an idiot child?"

"Did they say what's wrong with her?" I ask.

James nods his head no as he's biting his nails.

"Hello, are you all family?" a voice announces as a tall, pale-skinned man with bright green eyes, wearing a white medical coat, enters our mother's room.

Looking at each other with uncertainty, I quickly respond, "Yes, we are family."

"Well, it's unfortunate. Our good friend Mrs. Sally here is suffering from what is called dementia. Do you all know what dementia is?" the doctor asks as he places a hand on our mother's shoulder.

"Yes, I... I am familiar with what dementia is," I say. *But what on earth would make him think she has dementia?* Our mother tried to control people so much in her past that now she can't even control her own thoughts.

I couldn't feel sad. Not one tear could fall down my face. She did this to herself. Karma is real, and she thought she could attempt to kill my kids and get away with it; now look at her.

Our mother turned and looked at each of us. This crazy woman had no idea what was going on.

"I'm sorry kids. I... I'm sorry for everything. James, Alice, and Sarah. I'm truly sorry." Our mother said to each of us.

Our mouths dropped. Did she call each of us by our real names?

Lily-Ann wanted to keep up the appearance and didn't want anyone to find out who we were to her, but now the whole town would know. She can't even control her own mind. Dementia is in control of you now, Mother.

Even in her moment of weakness, I had thoughts of taking her pillow and suffocating her myself. This was the perfect moment. But I could see my sister and brother were completely confused.

At that moment, all I could do was laugh. My sister looked at me with tears pouring down her cheeks and said, "I know she was evil, but she's still our only mother, and you know she can die from this."

I understood what she was saying. She is right. Lily-Ann is our only mother, and she could die from dementia. Maybe my sister was feeling a little remorseful at that moment because we were getting ready to lose our supposed mother. Perhaps she was crying because she knew our lives were getting ready to change for the better.

Whatever the case may be, I took a deep breath and apologized for my behavior.

I looked at my sister and then at James. I then looked at Mr. Gerald, and suddenly, I couldn't hold it in any longer.

Mr. Gerald and I started laughing.

My sister swallowed what seemed to be a lump now in her throat, and James's mouth dropped.

My sister and brother were extremely confused at this point. I had to reveal to them what was going on. I went back to that night when my kids and Sam were chained up.

I began to explain to them at that moment; I knew killing our mother wasn't an option because our brother would kill Sam. I knew killing our brother wasn't an option because our mother would kill my kids. So I had to go along with her act no matter how long it took.

After that day, I started reading more about hypnosis and became very good friends with Mr. Gerald. Our mother was so big on having this perfect family and perfect life that I decided to get closer to our pretend dad.

I continued to explain how we got to this point. I informed them that at every opportunity, the kids and I would pay Mr. Gerald a visit and let him know what was going on. Little did we know the hypnosis had worn off on Mr. Gerald long ago.

Our mother was just wrapped up in herself. She missed the fact that Mr. Gerald's hypnosis wore off.

I informed them that the day I tried to trick my sister and our mother into going to the movies, he was peeking in on me when I found that secret door. He started developing his own questions.

With a smirk on my face, I revealed to them that while she was out trying to kill us, he was doing his research and found out about the hypnosis on everyone in the town. Our mother was so clueless.

He didn't want her to know, so he had to go along with her story about her whereabouts the day I tried to get into the house, pretending to search for my wallet. He knew he had to continue on as if he were still hypnotized, so he did everything she wanted him to do.

Mr. Gerald and I put together our own plan to get rid of this woman for good and free every one of this hypnosis she has them under. I decided to play family even more and start having dinners each week—several days a week, to be exact—to make Mother proud.

During these dinners, her plate was the only one that had a little extra ingredient. In every conversation, Mr. Gerald would mention little trigger words to make her start forgetting things like her nail appointment or hair appointment. Finally, he did what she did to us while she was out cold sleeping. He convinced her that she had dementia.

Someone can't control others' minds when theirs is also being controlled. So here we are; the people in the town are slowly coming out of their hypnosis while she is stuck in hers.

She will be medicated for the rest of her days, not knowing where she's at or who she is. She will no longer be that woman of mystery but a prune confined to a bed for the rest of her life.

Looking at my sister, I reminded her of my promise, which was to figure out a way out of this town one day. Our mother will no longer be able to control us, but we can now control her. She will not be able to murder another innocent person again. She made the biggest mistake the day she chained my kids up and tried to convince our brother to kill my only sister.

I had to think like our mother. I had to become crazy inside and out like our mother. It takes one to know one, and I had to become just like her to trap her.

Walking over to my brother, I gave him an ultimatum. He is my brother, after all. Who would I be to kill him or even let him spend the rest of his life in prison? I felt a little sympathy for him. I told him he had to leave this town. I didn't want him to breathe in the same state as me and my kids.

Reaching into my back pocket, I pulled out a

white envelope. Call me crazy, but I always kept this envelope on me. I wasn't sure when this day would come, and I wanted to ensure I was ready.

The envelope contained a one-way ticket anywhere in the United States and a wad of cash. I assured him if I ever found him, I would put a bullet in his head the same way he was willing to do our sister.

He gazed into my eyes; I think he could see my seriousness. He swallowed, reached out his hand, and snatched the envelope from me.

Taking one last look at each of us, almost as if he was a little sad that he could no longer be a part of our lives, James nodded his head and ran out the door.

My sister hugged me tightly. "Thank you Alice. Actually, thank you both," she said as she looked at Mr. Gerald and me.

I assured her these years did not go by in vain. Every day, I planned whether it was with Mr. Gerald or in my own head. I couldn't allow myself to watch my kids walk this earth and live this life. They only get one shot at being who they want to be, and hell will freeze over before I allow our mother to take that away from them.

Lily-Ann may have given birth to us, but she will never be my mother in my heart. She will never be my kid's grandmother. She thought she could keep us here in her prison. She thought she could change a town to be what she wanted it to be. She thought she could manipulate a man into being the perfect husband for her. But oh, Lily-Ann, this is the last night of your freedom.

I now have control over you. I am my mother's daughter, by the way. She will not get my sympathy. Before leaving the hospital, I knelt down next to Lily-Ann's bed and whispered in her ear as she did mine that night, and I said, "I know you didn't think it would be that easy to get away from me."

EPILOGUE

—

As I thought to myself how safe this town is now that a murderer is off the street, suddenly there was a loud alarm going off. I wasn't certain whose house it was coming from, but it was close enough as if it could have been my car alarm.

Curious, I peeked out the window to see whose alarm was going off. To my surprise, it was my car. I dashed out of bed and grabbed my robe. I wasn't concerned about robbers but more about waking the neighbors.

As I approached the front door, I thought of what I did to my brother Cameron the night I got into his house. I needed to create a distraction to get him out of the house. So I pulled on his car door handle, which caused the alarm to go off.

But I had to remind myself that we were all safe. Cameron was dead, James was long gone, and Lily-Ann was stuck in a facility for the rest of her days with dementia.

Chuckling at the silly thought of it being one of them, I shook my head to clear any negative thoughts. I knew we were all safe. Shelly Grove is probably the safest town in the state now that they're not around.

Stepping outside, I noticed something still didn't sit right with me. What would cause my car alarm to go off? I mean, there were no heavy winds to shake the car. Looking over at Mr. Geralds's house. You know, the one where my neighbor used to live before she was murdered? I felt that unsettling feeling again. The feeling as if she was here.

I couldn't blame her spirit for wanting to return and haunt the place. She was hypnotized and then murdered. If I were her, I would visit Lily-Ann every night, torturing her.

As I approached my car, I pressed the key fob to turn off the alarm. Checking inside and around the car, I saw no signs of someone trying to break in. I stood there puzzled, looking at my car. I couldn't understand what caused the alarm to go off.

The only answer I could think of was that it might have been an animal. We do have a few strays running around Shelly Grove, so it is very possible one of them may have brushed up against the car. But something still didn't feel right.

Just as I was about to accept the idea of it being an animal, suddenly, a strange sound came from the side of my house. It sounded as if something had hit the trashcans. I wasn't sure if it was an animal at this point, but I knew I needed to figure out what was back there.

Slowly walking to the side of the house, I looked over my shoulder to make sure no one else was outside. It was dark and quiet; you could hear a pin drop if you listened closely. Suddenly, it got cold, and that gut feeling I tend to get when something isn't right came upon me.

"Come on Alice, pull yourself together," I tell myself. *This is a safe town, and your mother is no longer in control,* I reminded myself as I approached the trashcans.

Slowly lifting the lid, I was startled by a raccoon as he jumped out of the trashcan. I swear it felt like my heart stopped beating at that moment. I had no idea what to expect, but I wasn't expecting a darn raccoon to jump out at me.

As I gathered myself, I stood there for a moment, chuckling. It felt like I was in a horror movie, and one of the creepy killers was about to jump out and get me. I just knew I was done for it. Shaking my head at the idea, I placed the lid back on the trashcan and headed towards the front of the house.

Laughing at what I just experienced, I had to remind myself that this town was not a horror movie. I had to remind myself that my neighbor was resting peacefully and had not returned to haunt the place. We have all been through a lot, so I also had to remind myself that things will take a while to feel completely normal again.

Before returning to the house, I wanted to recheck the car. At this point, I knew it was a raccoon, but you can never be too careful. So, I pulled on the handle to ensure all the doors were locked.

As I turned around to head towards the front door, I was startled by my brother James. He was standing there right before my eyes, dressed in all black. "You thought you could run me away, didn't you, sis?" He said to me right before hitting me upside my head with a crowbar.